Tears rimmed Hai t
want anyone to kn "

Pain sliced through Valerie. Was Hailey embarrassed by her? Was that why she didn't want people to know? "Why?"

"Because you're not my mom. I have a mom."

"Hailey—"

"Please don't tell anyone."

Hailey had been dealing with so much trauma. Would it be helpful to keep it a secret longer? Give her time to figure things out?

"I'll try to keep it quiet," Valerie said.

Hailey nodded as she left Valerie's car.

Wade was waiting for Valerie.

"Sorry," Valerie said. "I promise I'm not usually late."

He grinned and she couldn't help but return his smile. He had been a bright spot over the past weekend— the only one she'd had.

"No need to apologize," he said. "It'll take you two some time to figure things out."

"Thank you for understanding. You don't know how much that means to me."

She'd never noticed how blue his eyes were or how his mouth tilted at a charming angle when he smiled.

But she had given up on a happily-ever-after.

No matter how cute or understanding Wade Griffin might be, it was best if she kept him at a distance.

Gabrielle Meyer lives in central Minnesota on the banks of the Mississippi River with her husband and four young children. As an employee of the Minnesota Historical Society, she fell in love with the rich history of her state and enjoys writing fictional stories inspired by real people and events. Gabrielle can be found at www.gabriellemeyer.com, where she writes about her passion for history, Minnesota and her faith.

Books by Gabrielle Meyer

Love Inspired

A Mother's Secret
Unexpected Christmas Joy
A Home for Her Baby
Snowed in for Christmas
Fatherhood Lessons
The Soldier's Baby Promise
The Baby Proposal
The Baby Secret
Her Summer Refuge
Her Christmas Secret

Visit the Author Profile page at LoveInspired.com for more titles.

Her Christmas Secret

GABRIELLE MEYER

LOVE INSPIRED
INSPIRATIONAL ROMANCE

LOVE INSPIRED®
INSPIRATIONAL ROMANCE

Recycling programs
for this product may
not exist in your area.

ISBN-13: 978-1-335-90458-4

Her Christmas Secret

Love Inspired
22 Adelaide St. West, 41st Floor
Toronto, Ontario M5H 4E3, Canada
www.LoveInspired.com

Printed in U.S.A.

And above all things have fervent charity among yourselves: for charity shall cover the multitude of sins.
—*1 Peter* 4:8

For David, my hero.

Chapter One

If Valerie Wilmington wasn't so happy to finally have her own house, she would have dreaded the fall cleanup. Her new yard was bigger than she had anticipated when she saw the pictures online, but it was beautiful and full of trees—which meant there were a lot of leaves. Red oak, orange maple, and yellow ash littered her yard and offered a mosaic of autumn colors. The late November weather was cold, and she should have had the leaves picked up sooner, but she'd been too busy adjusting to her new job as the principal at the Timber Falls Christian School.

A sharp wind blew against her as she put the last pile of leaves in the garbage bin she'd been using to haul to the city compost pile. The sun was starting to fall toward the horizon, prompting her to pull her phone out of her back pocket and look at the time.

Twenty minutes to three.

Good. Just enough time to change and get to the school to meet with the contractor about the leak that had ruined the kindergarten classroom.

She put away her rake, shovel and garbage bin in the detached garage at the back of her property and then went into the house. It was Saturday, but it was the only day the contractor could meet with her. She didn't mind. She'd probably end up at the school sometime today anyway. There was always something that needed to be done.

Her house was an American Foursquare with white siding, a covered front porch and a third-floor dormer. It was over a hundred and thirty years old and full of so much charm, she had fallen in love with it the moment she saw it online. She'd purchased it sight unseen and was so thankful she loved it even more in person. The previous owners had done a lot of work to modernize the kitchen and bathroom, but the rest of the house looked original. One of her favorite features was a small fireplace in the cozy little den, tucked into the corner of the main floor. On cold evenings like this one, she loved to light a fire, fill up a mug of steaming tea or hot chocolate and read for hours on end.

Her toy poodle, Annabelle, greeted her at the back door with an excited wag of her tail. "I'm going to be late," she said to Annabelle as she stopped to pet the three-year-old dog. "And Mr. Griffin won't like that."

Valerie went up the steps to the second floor and was just slipping into a clean pair of jeans and a blouse when the front doorbell rang. She wished there was someone else to get the door, but since she lived alone, there was no one else but her.

With a sigh, she left her bedroom and went back down the steps, taking her blond hair out of the ponytail it had been in. The front door opened onto the covered porch, but her visitors had let themselves into the porch and were standing on the other side of the door. A window at the top of the door let Valerie know who had arrived— and her heart fell.

She pulled the door open and stared at her mother—and her ten-year-old daughter, Hailey.

A dozen different emotions fought for attention. Surprise, fear, uncertainty…and joy.

"Mom," Valerie said, breathless from surprise. "What are you doing here?"

She hadn't seen her mom since last Christmas—almost a year ago. It was the only time that she saw her mom and Hailey. It had been the simplest way to deal with the situation since Hailey had been born—though it had never been easy. The only way her mom would agree to raise Hailey when Valerie gave birth to her at the age of eighteen was to say that Hailey was her child.

To this day, Hailey believed Valerie was her sister—not her mother.

"Hello, Valerie," her mom said. "May we come in?"

"Yes." Valerie moved aside, and for the first time, she noticed the four large suitcases on the porch with them. "What's going on?"

Hailey was ten years old and looked just like Valerie had at that age. Straight blond hair, big blue eyes and a button nose. She didn't look anything like Valerie's high school boyfriend, Soren. He had dark brown hair and eyes.

But Valerie pushed thoughts of Soren away. She hadn't seen him in ten years. He'd broken up with her the moment he learned she was pregnant and refused to even discuss the baby. He had wanted nothing to do with her or Hailey. In the moment when she needed him most, he'd broken her heart and abandoned her.

"Hi, Hailey," Valerie said, offering a smile, though her heart was pounding.

"Hi." Hailey glanced up at Valerie, shy and uncertain. She held her mom's hand and stood close to her side. They'd only seen each other ten times in Hailey's life— the day she was born and at each Christmas holiday since then. No wonder the little girl was nervous to be at Valerie's house for the first time.

Her mom had worked two jobs as a single parent while raising Valerie. Thankfully, Valerie had flourished as a student and had been the valedictorian of her class—but what none of her classmates knew was that she was six months pregnant with Hailey under her graduation gown. She'd done a good job hiding the pregnancy until summer break and then she and her mom had left their small suburban town in Minnesota and moved to

Saint Paul. It had been easy enough for her mom to say that Hailey was her baby and for Hailey to head away to college in Wisconsin.

What had been hard was living with the ache of guilt and shame Valerie had felt.

"You have a beautiful home, Valerie," her mom said as she looked around the spacious living room with its tall windows, arched doorways and hardwood floors. "I'm happy for you."

"Thank you." Valerie frowned. Her mom was acting like they were just in the neighborhood and decided to stop in. Yet— her mom and Hailey lived in Saint Paul, which was over a hundred miles southeast of Timber Falls. This visit had to be deliberate. But why? Her mom had never sought her out without warning before— and never with four suitcases. "What's going on, Mom?"

"Can we have a seat?"

Valerie glanced at the wall clock. It was three, which meant she would be late to meet the contractor—something she hated. Being late meant being selfish of someone else's time. His number was on a piece of paper on her desk at work, so she had no way of contacting him.

She'd have to apologize later.

Valerie motioned to the two couches facing each other. "Sit wherever you'd like."

Her mom took a seat and Hailey sat close by her side.

Valerie sat on the opposite couch with the coffee table between them and clasped her hands, waiting.

The quiet in the room lengthened as her mom studied Valerie. Finally, her mom said, "I told Hailey the truth."

Valerie stared at her mom, unsure she'd heard her correctly. "The truth?"

"Yes. About you—and her—and us."

"What are you saying?" Panic raced through Valerie, making her heart pound. Had her mom told Hailey that Valerie was her biological mother? But why would she do that without consulting Valerie? Why would she do it at all?

Her mom took her time to answer and finally said, "I met someone."

A strange quiet filled the air. Valerie shook her head. "I don't understand."

"I'm getting remarried—tomorrow, in Las Vegas," her mom said. "Lyle and I met a couple months ago at the grocery store, and we started to date. He is a retiree and spends his summers in Minnesota and his winters in Arizona at a gated retirement community. When he asked me to marry him, I knew I had to decide." Her blue eyes, so much like Valerie's and Hailey's, were filled with pain. "I've spent my entire life sacrificing for others. And I haven't complained. It's been a fulfilling and rewarding life. But I'm tired, Valerie. And I don't want to be lonely for the rest of my life. Lyle is a good man, and he wants to make me happy."

"What are you saying?" Valerie asked again, trying to understand as Hailey's gaze was on her. Everything felt like it was suffocating her. Her clothes, the air—the look in Hailey's eyes.

"I'm saying that children cannot live in the retirement community, and, to be honest, Lyle isn't in a position to help raise Hailey. He's ten years older than me." She paused for a heartbeat and then continued. "A few weeks ago, I told Hailey the truth. We've been working through the pain that she has had to deal with, but she understands why we chose to tell her that I was her mother and not her grandmother. And she understands that it's best for her to live with you now."

"Live with me?" Valerie felt like she was dreaming—like she was sitting outside herself watching all of this unfold.

"That's why I've brought all her things—at least, most of them." Her mom offered a sad smile. "I know I shouldn't have sprung this on you, but I didn't want you to try to talk me out of it. This will be best for all of us. Maybe a little hard in the beginning, but in the end, we'll realize it was supposed to work out this way."

"Work out?" Valerie felt silly, as if she couldn't comprehend what was happening.

"I explained to Hailey that you gave birth to her right after you graduated high school," her mom said. "And I wanted you to go to college and make something of yourself, because I was never given that option since I had you at the age of eighteen. When she was born, I thought I was doing the best thing for all of us, but I didn't realize that I was keeping both of you from the most important relationship of your life. You two need to know each other—so that's why I brought Hailey here."

Valerie scooted to the edge of her couch, feeling desperate. When she had found out she was pregnant, her world had crashed down around her. But when her mom offered her a new start, she had promised herself she'd never make the same mistake again. She kept her boyfriends at a distance—which meant they didn't stick around for long. But that was for the best. Nothing was out of place in her life. She was disciplined, organized and diligent. She had set goals for herself and stuck to them. A five-year plan and then a ten-year plan—which had included becoming a principal. But her fifteen-year plan didn't involve raising a daughter. "I—I just started a new job. No one knows I have a daughter. What will I tell them?"

Her mom stood and put her hand on Valerie's cheek. "You'll figure it out, honey. I should have let you figure it out ten years ago."

Anger and fear tore at Valerie's chest. Her mother should have at least given her time to process this before bringing Hailey. "How could you do this to us?"

Tears fell down her mom's cheeks as she shook her head. "I don't want to hurt either of you—but there's no other way." She turned to Hailey, who was crying, though she seemed resigned. She'd had time to accept this. "I'm leaving now," her mom said as she reached for Hailey to give her a hug.

"Wait." Valerie was trying to get her thoughts to catch up. "I don't have a room set up for her, I don't know what kind of food she likes, or her medical information, or anything."

"I wrote everything down," her mom said as she pulled away from Hailey. "I have her medical and school records in a folder in one of the suitcases. Whatever I haven't covered, she can tell you. She's smart and confident and knows what she likes and dislikes—just like you."

Valerie stared at her daughter and Hailey stared back.

"Mom," Valerie tried again as her mother moved to the front door. "You're leaving? Just like that?"

"I don't want to make this harder on Hailey than it needs to be. We said our goodbyes and she understands what's happening."

"What about me?" Valerie asked, feeling like a helpless ten-year-old herself. "I don't understand why you're doing this."

Her mom leaned forward and kissed Valerie's cheek. "You're a smart, educated woman. You deal with children for a living. You'll figure it out. Goodbye, Valerie. I love you." She looked at Hailey. "And I love you, too."

"Bye," Hailey said, quietly.

Valerie couldn't process what was happening as her mother opened the front door and slipped outside, closing it behind her.

For a heartbeat, Valerie just stared at the door. But then she opened it and walked out onto the porch.

Her mom was already on the sidewalk, moving toward a pickup truck where a man waited for her.

"That's Lyle," Hailey said beside Valerie. "They're flying to Las Vegas tonight to get married and then he's taking her to Arizona."

Valerie looked down at Hailey and she looked back at Valerie.

What in the world were they going to do?

* * *

Wade Griffin was rarely on time for anything in his life—but he had made sure he was at the Timber Falls Christian School a few minutes before three, because he knew the principal was a stickler for punctuality.

Yet, as Wade sat in his truck in the parking lot with his ten-year-old daughter, Isabel, and his seven-year-old son, Brayden, Miss Wilmington was nowhere to be found. She was already twenty minutes late.

Maybe she forgot, though he doubted it. He'd met her at his kids' open house and spoken to her once about the project at the school, but both times he had sensed that she was disciplined and precise. Not someone who would be late.

"I'm hungry," Brayden said from the back seat of the king cab.

"We just ate lunch a couple hours ago," Wade told him. "You can hold out for supper, buddy."

"But I don't like supper."

"You don't know what we're having."

"I don't like anything we have for supper."

Wade glanced in the rearview mirror and said, "What if I told you Grammy is coming over and she's bringing your favorite?"

"Lasagna?" Brayden asked with a big grin.

"Yep."

"Yay!" Both Issy and Brayden cheered.

Issy was sitting next to Brayden. Her dark brown hair and brown eyes reminded him of his ex-wife, Amber. Issy was a miniature version of her mom who was now living in Los Angeles with her new boyfriend, trying to break into the movies.

Wade didn't let himself think about Amber often. The lies she had told him had nearly destroyed him. She'd been gone for six years, and he still struggled to trust people and let them get close. It was easier to focus on being a dad and working for his father's construction company than it was to think about all the disappointments in his thirty-two years of life.

"Where is the principal?" Wade asked as he looked out the window of his truck at the empty parking lot. "Does she think my time isn't as valuable as hers?"

"Daddy," Issy said in a singsong voice. "If you don't have anything nice to say, don't say anything at all."

Wade briefly closed his eyes and took a deep breath. "You're right, Issy. Thanks for the reminder."

His kids often reminded him of the lessons he was trying to teach them.

"Maybe she forgot," Brayden offered.

"Maybe." Wade looked at the clock again. "I need to get into the school to look at the damage from the broken pipe if I'm going to start working on it on Monday."

"Let's go to her house," Issy suggested. "And see why she's not here."

"Even if I knew where she lived—" Wade paused as he saw a car pull into the parking lot. "It looks like she just got here."

He didn't usually take his kids to job-sites with him, but this was their school, and it was Saturday. As a single dad, he had little choice.

The black Toyota Camry pulled into the spot next to him and Miss Wilmington got out of the driver's side, looking frazzled and panicky.

Wade frowned. Every time he'd seen her, she was composed, confident and calm.

One of the back doors of the Camry opened and a little girl got out. She had blond hair and looked like a miniature version of the principal.

"Does your principal have a daughter?" he asked Issy and Brayden.

"No," Issy said. "I don't think so."

Wade got out of his truck with a pad of paper and a pencil, trying not to let his frustration show.

"I'm so sorry I'm late," Miss Wilmington said as she pulled a set of keys from her purse and started to move toward the school door, barely looking at him. "A—a family emergency came up."

Any irritation Wade felt vanished when he saw the turmoil in her gaze. He had a feeling that *family emergency* was an understatement. She looked distressed. "It's okay," he said. "The kids and I were fine waiting."

"Daddy," Issy said—but he put his hand on his daughter's shoulder to silence her. She was probably going to say it wasn't okay to tell a fib.

"Thank you," Miss Wilmington said as she fumbled with the keys and then glanced at the little girl.

Issy and the girl looked each other over. They were complete opposites in looks but were about the same height and age.

"This is my—ahh—" Miss Wilmington paused.

"I'm her sister," the little girl said. "I'm Hailey."

Sister? Wade frowned. The age gap was remarkable, but their looks were so similar, he wasn't surprised they were related.

"I'm Isabel," Issy said. "Will you come to school here?"

Hailey looked at Miss Wilmington with a question in her eyes.

"Yes," Miss Wilmington said without hesitation. "She'll start Monday. Her arrival was very unexpected, so we have a lot of decisions to make—but we know she'll go to school here."

Was that the family emergency? The unexpected arrival of her little sister? No wonder the principal was frazzled. Had something horrible happened to her parents?

"I hope everything's okay with your family," Wade said.

Miss Wilmington nodded. "Everything's fine. We just have some adjusting to do. Let's get into the building so you can get on with your day."

Wade and the kids followed her into the school. The large building had been added to the back of the Timber Falls Community Church three years ago and was a perfect addition to their small town. Wade hadn't hesitated to enroll Issy for second grade when the school opened. He'd appreciated her teachers and the last principal—but this new one was still a mystery to him. She seemed kind and caring—but she was also distant and a little cold.

"The water pipe broke in the kindergarten classroom on Thursday night," Miss Wilmington said as she turned on the lights and led the way. "We were able to get all the furniture and school supplies out yesterday, but the carpet and some of the Sheetrock will need to be replaced. We're hoping the project won't take too long, since the kindergartners will be using the staff conference room until they can get back into their classroom."

"It shouldn't take more than a week or two," he said. "Though that's only a guess, since I haven't seen the room yet."

The kindergarten classroom was the closest to the main office, which was near the front door. Miss Wilmington unlocked the classroom door and flipped on the lights.

"We had a cleaning service come in yesterday and suck up all the water," she said. "But we'll need your crew to remove the carpet and the damaged Sheetrock. I'm not even sure what else needs to happen."

Wade entered and looked around. "The cabinets on the floor might need to be replaced, too."

Miss Wilmington sighed. "I hadn't noticed that."

"They look like they're standard size. We should be able to replace them without any trouble. Might take a little more time, though."

"That's what I don't want to hear." Every time Wade had seen the principal, she'd been in business attire. Skirts, suit coats, high heels, button-down shirts. Now, she was wearing jeans and a blouse with a wool jacket that tied at the waist. She was pretty, in a kind of girl-next-door way. He'd noticed right away, but her cool exterior had made him push aside those thoughts.

Now, frazzled, in casual clothes, with

her hair in kind of a mess around her face, she looked cute. Approachable.

Hailey was quiet as she looked around the room and then studied her older sister. There was something about the pair that struck him as strange. Did they know each other very well? They almost appeared like strangers.

Or was that just Miss Wilmington's personality? Was she cool and aloof with her sister, too?

"I'll take a few pictures and get some measurements," Wade said, looking back at the room. "I'll plan to be here by six thirty on Monday morning. My crew will get here by seven."

"Wonderful. I'll be here at six thirty to open the school for you. Thank you for the quick action. I'm sure we probably pulled you off another job to do this one."

"It's no trouble at all." Which wasn't exactly true. He was a contractor for his dad's company—and his dad had several crews. When Wade said the kids' school needed help, his dad had shifted some things around and given the job to Wade—though there had been a lot of grumbling and complaining on his dad's part. They were busy this time of year, trying to wrap up projects before the snow started to fall. It was harder to come by work in the winter, though, so they would take what they could get now.

"Can we play on the playground while we wait?" Brayden asked Wade.

"I don't see why not," he said.

"Want to come with us?" Issy asked Hailey.

Hailey glanced at Miss Wilmington, a shy curiosity in her gaze.

"Go ahead," the principal said. "But stick together."

"Come on." Issy took Hailey's hand and said, "I think we're going to be good friends."

Hailey smiled and nodded, a bit of the shyness wearing off.

"Keep your coat buttoned up," Miss

Wilmington said. "And be careful on the monkey bars. Don't talk to any strangers." She followed the kids out into the hallway, calling orders as they went.

Wade started to take pictures of the damage as Miss Wilmington came back into the room and walked to the window where she had a view of the playground.

"I take it her arrival was a surprise?" he asked.

He wasn't sure if she was going to answer, but then she finally said, "The biggest surprise of my life."

There was something deep and complicated in her simple response.

He'd had a few of those kind of surprises in his life as well.

Chapter Two

Hailey was quiet in the back seat as Valerie drove toward her house an hour later. She glanced in the rearview mirror, watching Hailey take in the small town. They passed the historic courthouse with its tall clock tower, and drove down Second Street with all the old, beautiful homes. It must be strange for her to leave Saint Paul, one of the biggest cities in Minnesota, and come to a little community like Timber Falls. There were no big shopping malls, concert venues or skyscrapers. The heaviest traffic happened when the schools let out at three, or a train was longer than normal and the cars were backed up for a couple of minutes along Broadway. It was a charming community with historic buildings, quaint parks and the Mississippi River running straight through the heart of the town.

Neither one said a word as Valerie turned into the alley behind her house and parked the car in the detached garage.

What could she say to her daughter? Even if she'd had weeks to prepare, she didn't know. There was so much to tell her—yet her mind was blank.

They got out of the car and Valerie closed the garage door as they left the side entrance.

"Are you mad?" Hailey asked as she looked up at Valerie.

"Mad? Who would I be made at?"

"Mom or me."

Valerie stopped on the back sidewalk and shook her head. "I'm not mad at you, Hailey. You're not to blame for any of this. Do you understand?"

"That's what Mom told me, too. Or should I call her Grandma?" She wrinkled up her face. "That's weird."

"It doesn't matter what you call her," Valerie said with a sigh. "She's the only mom you've ever had." *Until now,* she wanted to add, but it was still strange to think of herself as a mom. "Come on. Let's get inside and make supper."

Valerie opened the door onto the back porch and then the kitchen. Annabelle was at the door, ready to greet them.

"You have a dog?" Hailey asked excitedly as she got on the floor to pet Annabelle. "What's her name?"

"Annabelle."

"Hello, Annabelle," Hailey said with a giggle. "Mom wouldn't let me get a dog, but I've always wanted one."

A smile tilted Valerie's lips for the first time since her mom's unexpected arrival. "Now you have one." It seemed weird to think about Hailey being a part of her life full-time. It had been a hard enough transition to get a puppy three years ago. But a little girl?

"Can you take her outside?" Valerie asked. "She needs to go potty."

"Sure." Hailey jumped up and called for Annabelle to follow her into the backyard. "Will she run off?"

"No. She stays in the yard, but you still need to keep an eye on her."

Hailey's laughter filled Valerie's heart with a strange ache—and she suddenly realized how much she had missed that laughter. She'd missed a lot of things in Hailey's life, but it wasn't something she had allowed herself to ponder before. It hurt too much.

She stood at the kitchen sink and looked out the window to the backyard as she watched Annabelle and Hailey play. She hadn't seen Annabelle so excited or active before. Perhaps the dog had been missing out, too.

Valerie turned back to her kitchen and stared at it for a minute, trying to decide what to make for supper. What did ten-year-old girls like to eat? As much time as she spent with children, she didn't know much about taking care of one. She knew how to run a school, how to meet state standards, how to hire and fire employees, and discipline children in a school setting—but when it came to feeding them? She was at a loss.

The school lunches weren't much help, either. Valerie wasn't a big fan of what they provided for the children. Pizza, chicken nuggets, hamburgers or fish sticks. None of them looked appetizing or nutritious.

She surveyed at her weekly menu and stared at Saturday's supper. Spicy Tuna Sushi Roll. She loved to cook and often tried new recipes with complicated ingredients on the weekends just for fun. But would Hailey like raw tuna?

As Valerie began to take out the ingredients, she kept an eye on Hailey and Annabelle. Hailey had found one of Annabelle's balls and was playing fetch with her. Hailey's cheeks were growing pink from the cold, but she seemed happy to stay outside.

Finally, as Valerie was slicing the ahi tuna into long, thin strips, Hailey came inside with Annabelle. She was breathless and her blond hair was windblown, but both the dog and little girl seemed happy.

Hailey's smile fell as she looked at the ingredients for the sushi on the kitchen island. "What's that?"

"It's our supper. We're having sushi."

"Sushi?" Hailey's frown deepened. "What's that?"

"It's a Japanese dish with rice, vegetables and fish."

"Fish?" Hailey made a gagging noise. "I don't like fish."

Disappointment weighed on Valerie. "Not even tuna?"

Hailey shrugged. "I like tuna sandwiches."

"That's all this is," Valerie said, indicating the fish on the cutting board. "It's tuna."

Hailey came closer to the counter and sniffed at the fish. "That doesn't look like tuna."

"It is."

Hailey glanced up at Valerie to see if she was teasing.

"And this is just rice," Valerie continued, pointing to the container where the rice was waiting. She'd added a mixture of vinegar, sugar and salt to it, but that shouldn't bother Hailey. "And here are some carrots, cucumbers and avocados," she continued. "They're just cut into little strips."

"Okay," Hailey said tentatively.

Valerie worked for a few more minutes cutting everything up as Hailey sat on a stool and watched. "After supper, we'll get your things brought up to the room that you'll be using."

Hailey nodded.

"Did Mom sell her house in Saint Paul?"

"She's trying to." Hailey lifted a shoulder. "Lyle's rich, so it doesn't matter."

Valerie nibbled her bottom lip. She and

her mother had never been close, but after Hailey was born, they had become almost like strangers. She wasn't surprised that her mother had met and fallen in love with someone and not told her until now.

Neither one spoke for a few more minutes and then Valerie asked Hailey a question that had been bothering her. "Why did you tell Isabel Griffin that I was your sister? Why didn't you just tell her that I am your mom? We can't keep it hidden forever."

Hailey didn't look at Valerie as she shrugged. "It feels weird."

Valerie nodded. "It does feel weird." She stopped slicing the jalapeño and studied Hailey. "I'm sorry—about everything."

Hailey met her gaze, her blue eyes so innocent and beautiful. "I know. Mom is sorry, too."

"We never meant to hurt you."

"Who is my dad?"

The question took Valerie by surprise, and she blinked a few times. She had been dishonest with Hailey long enough. She decided not to keep anything from her again. "His name is Soren Johnson, and he was my boyfriend when I was eighteen. He played football and basketball and was really smart. Everyone liked him. He got good grades and was involved in a lot of activities in school."

"Does he know about me?" Hailey's questions were raw and vulnerable, but she didn't look uncomfortable asking Valerie.

"Yes. When I found out I was pregnant, he was the first person I told." Valerie looked down at the counter, trying not to let her emotions get the better of her. She prided herself on always being calm and confident, especially in front of children. "He was surprised and really scared—just like me. But he wasn't ready to be a dad—and I wasn't ready to be a mom. We were very young, and we both had big dreams. So, he decided to break up with me and I didn't force him to be part of our lives."

"And Mom said she'd take me," Hailey finished for her. "So you could go to college."

Valerie nodded, but quickly added, "None of it is your fault, Hailey."

"I know." Her simple answer told Valerie that her mom had done a good job explaining all this already.

But tears gathered in Hailey's eyes and rolled down her cheeks.

"What's wrong?" Valerie asked, coming around the counter as she wiped her hands on a dish towel.

"I'm scared," Hailey said. "I don't want to live here."

Valerie had never touched Hailey. Not after she gave birth to her or at any of the Christmases they had shared together. Her mom had never been very affectionate with Valerie, either.

But Valerie wanted to hug Hailey—wanted to pull her into her arms and promise her that everything was going to be okay, even if she wasn't sure it would be.

Tenderly, Valerie put her arm around Hailey's shoulders and said, "I know. I'm scared, too."

"You are?"

Valerie nodded. "I'm scared that I'm going to be a bad mom—and that you're not going to like me."

Hailey wiped her cheeks and shook her head. "I like you."

"You do?"

Nodding, Hailey sniffed. "And I like Annabelle, too."

Valerie smiled, but then grew serious. "I promise you that I'm going to do everything I can to make you happy, Hailey. I know all of this is scary and you have a lot of new things to get used to, but we're doing this together, okay? You're not alone. You have me and Annabelle."

Hailey's smile returned and she nodded, but then she looked at the food and said, "Can I have real tuna?"

Valerie chuckled and pulled away from her daughter. "I'll see if I have some canned tuna for you."

It wasn't going to be easy, but Valerie had never let anything get in the way of her goals. And now, she had a new one. She was going to be a good mom.

She just wished she wasn't so nervous that she'd fail.

Wade entered Timber Falls Community Church on Sunday morning with Issy and Brayden at his side. Their energy was exhausting, but for some reason, on Sunday mornings, it felt twice as draining.

"Church starts in fifteen minutes," he called to his kids as they ran off to find their friends. "I expect you in the sanctuary in ten."

His children knew the drill, though it wasn't unusual for one of them to get sidetracked and forget to come when the worship leader started to sing.

"There you are," his mom said as he left the back entrance and came into the fellowship hall just outside the doors to the sanctuary. "I forgot my lasagna pan at your house last night. Did you remember to bring it?"

"No." Wade shook his head. As if that was all he had to remember. "I'm happy that I remembered to tell the kids to put on their shoes and jackets before we left the house this morning."

"That's too bad." She scrunched up her face, as if in thought. "I suppose I can use my second-best baking dish for the casserole I'm making for Mary Lou. She's down with a cold and the other ladies and I are bringing her meals this week. But I hate to give her my second best. You know how she can be."

He did know. His mom's friends were a group of ladies who were affectionately known as the Church Ladies. They meant well, though they could be pushy and exasperating at times. Mary Lou Caruthers was a bit of a ringleader, though Mrs. Evans, Mrs. Topper, and even Mrs. Anderson could cause their fair share of trouble without Mrs. Caruthers. They had been trying to pair him up with some of the single women in the church for years. But he had no desire to get romantically involved again. It hurt too much the first time.

Miss Wilmington entered through the front doors, Hailey at her side. Both looked around the fellowship hall nervously, as if they were trying to be inconspicuous—though they would no doubt draw attention. Miss Wilmington had faithfully attended church each week since she'd come to Timber Falls at the end of August to take over the school. But the addition of a little girl at her side would make people curious.

"Who is that child with the principal?" his mom asked as she moved her head to get a better view. She made no attempt to look inconspicuous herself.

"That's Miss Wilmington's sister," Wade said.

"Sister?" His mom frowned. "That little girl? It's an age gap if I've ever seen one."

"I think Hailey's arrival was unexpected.

Miss Wilmington seemed a little rattled yesterday when I met her at the school to look at the project in the kindergarten room."

His mom's gaze returned to Wade and a new light twinkled in her eyes. "You've been talking to Miss Wilmington?"

"About the project—yes." He knew that matchmaking look. "Nothing more."

"Why not? She's single, you're single."

"Mom—"

"Oh, let me have some fun," she said.

"Even if I was interested in a relationship again, Miss Wilmington is not my type."

"Why not?" she asked, incredulous.

"She's aloof, for one thing—and organized and punctual."

"All the more reason you need her in your life." She took his hand. "Let's go meet the little girl."

"I've met her."

She tugged his hand and, for some reason, he didn't protest.

Miss Wilmington was wearing a pair of black pants with a gray sweater. Her blond hair was styled today, and she didn't look as frazzled, though she still seemed uncertain and less confident. Hailey stood beside her in a dress, looking around the church like it was the first time she'd ever been to one.

"Hello, Miss Wilmington," his mom said as she finally let go of Wade's hand.

"Please," she said, "call me Valerie. It's nice to see you again."

Wade had heard her name before, but not from her own lips. He liked it. He hadn't known many Valeries.

Valerie glanced at Wade and offered him a smile. "Hello."

"Hi."

Issy must have been watching because she ran up to Wade's side and said, "Hi, Hailey! Want to get a doughnut with me?"

Hailey grinned and then looked at Valerie.

"You deserve it after the tuna fiasco last

night," Valerie said. "But be back in about five minutes so we can find a spot to sit."

"You can sit with us," Issy said to Valerie and then Hailey. "We always sit on the right side toward the back."

"Can we sit with Issy?" Hailey asked Valerie.

Valerie looked at Wade, a question in her pretty blue eyes.

"Of course," Wade said. "Anyone is welcome to sit with us."

As the girls ran off, his mom looked from Wade to Valerie, a self-satisfied smile on her lips, as if she'd just coordinated the perfect match.

"Who is that adorable child?" his mom asked Valerie.

"Oh—that's Hailey," she said, smiling awkwardly.

"Her sister," Wade told his mother impatiently, since he'd already explained.

"Your sister?" his mom asked. "Were you expecting her?"

"No." This time, Valerie's response was certain, but she gave no other information.

"I hope your parents are okay," his mom said, her eyebrows coming together with worry. "They didn't die, did they?"

Valerie didn't seem like the kind of person who shared her private life openly with others. And she proved that to be true as she smiled kindly at Wade's mom and said, "It's been a difficult twenty-four hours, as you can imagine. I'd like Hailey to acclimate as quickly as she can, so I'm not comfortable talking about the difficult situation. I hope you understand."

His mom opened her mouth to speak again—but Wade responded instead. "We do understand." He looked at his mom. "And we'll respect Miss Wilmington's privacy, won't we?"

His mom lifted an eyebrow at him, but she eventually nodded. "Of course. I'm sorry to have pried."

He knew she wasn't sorry, but it was the proper thing to say.

"Oh, there's Roberta," his mom said. "I'll chat with you two later."

Mom ran off to talk to her friend Mrs. Anderson, and he had a sneaking suspicion they were going to discuss Valerie and Hailey—and might even throw in his name for good measure.

"Sorry about that," Wade said to Valerie. "She means well—I think."

"I know." Valerie had always seemed busy and distracted when he'd seen her before. He'd watched her from a distance but liked that up close she didn't seem so unapproachable. "If I was her, I'd have a lot of questions, too."

"It can be tough raising a child on your own." He shook his head. "I know it all too well. The last thing you need or want is advice or difficult questions."

She looked at him—really looked, and said, "I'm sorry. I guess I hadn't realized that you were raising your kids on your own. I'm still trying to get to know everyone."

"That's okay. It's just been me and the kids for six years now. Their mom is in California. I've been a single dad for most of their lives."

Valerie nodded. "I have a steep learning curve ahead of me."

"Will Hailey be staying with you permanently? If you don't mind me asking."

"That's okay." She nodded. "Yes. I think this is a permanent situation."

"If you need anything—even if you're just curious what kind of pain reliever takes down a fever, I'm happy to help. I learned the hard way for a lot of things and if I can ease someone else's difficulty, I'm happy to do it."

She offered him a smile, revealing two dimples in her cheeks. They took him by surprise and made his pulse tick a little higher.

"Thank you," she said. "I appreciate that."

Issy and Hailey ran through the fellowship hall on their way to the sanctuary, Brayden not far behind.

"It looks like those two have become instant friends," Wade said.

"I wish it was that easy as adults—don't you?"

Wade looked back at Valerie and smiled. "I do too." He motioned toward the sanctuary. "Should we join them?"

She nodded, and then leaned a little close as she whispered, "Maybe I can avoid other prying church ladies if I sit next to you." But then she looked up, her blue eyes growing wide. "Sorry, I didn't mean to imply your mother—"

Wade laughed and shook his head. "Don't worry. I'm the first person to admit my mom likes to pry. She's in good company with Mrs. Caruthers, Mrs. Evans, Mrs. Anderson, and several others." His laughter quieted, but his smile remained. "I'll do my best to protect you—but I can't make any promises. They outnumber us."

Valerie's laughter was bright and charming—and he realized he had been all wrong about her.

Maybe adults could make friends as fast as children did if they wanted to.

And Wade suddenly wanted to very much.

Chapter Three

Valerie woke up on Monday morning before her alarm and the first thing she thought about was Hailey. The tuna on Saturday night had been a disaster, so Valerie had scrapped Sunday's menu and they had ordered a pizza. Thankfully, she made her menu plan each Sunday afternoon, so she and Hailey had sat down at the dining-room table after church and put together a menu that they both liked. Then, they had gone shopping and there was food in the house that Hailey would eat.

They had spent most of Sunday evening organizing Hailey's bedroom, which was the room right next to Valerie's. It even had a connecting door since it was probably a nursery at one point. The beadboard on the walls was a creamy yellow and the trim around the tall windows and doors was white. A built-in closet spanned one side of the room and polished maple floors gleamed under the floral rug.

Now, as Valerie lay in bed, apprehension started to wind around her heart. A laid-back Sunday was one thing—returning to daily life with a child was going to be another. Especially when she had to explain who the child was to the school and community. What would they think of her when they learned she had given birth to a child at the age of eighteen? Would they judge her? Think less of her? Possibly ask her to resign?

That last thought wasn't likely, but it still worried her.

Annabelle used to sleep with Valerie, but the last two nights, she'd slept with Hailey in her bedroom. Valerie didn't mind. It seemed to ease Hailey's anxiety about living in a new house. But she knew Annabelle would need to go outside and Hailey would need to wake up if they were going to get ready, eat breakfast and get to the school to open it up at six thirty for Wade.

Just thinking about him made her heart beat a little harder. He'd been so kind at church the day before, shielding her from his mom's questions, offering to help as she navigated raising Hailey on her own. She'd been surprised to learn he was single—and then surprised again at how much it pleased her to know he wasn't married. She hated that he thought Hailey was her sister—but that couldn't be helped right now.

Valerie slowly opened the connecting door between her room and Hailey's room.

The sun was not yet up, so the room was still dark. But Valerie didn't need the light to know how the room was situated. It had been one of two guest bedrooms on the second floor, though she'd never had use of them. A full-size bed with a white comforter sat against the far wall and a white bureau stood opposite. Flowing white curtains at the windows allowed natural sunlight to pour in during the day and offered a bit of privacy at night.

Annabelle woke up and jumped off Hailey's bed, her collar jingling and her claws tapping on the floor as she ran to Valerie.

"Annabelle?" Hailey asked in a sleepy voice.

"It's just me," Valerie said. "I'm taking Annabelle out to go potty."

"Do I have to get up?"

"In a little bit. I'll come back when it's time."

"Okay," Hailey mumbled as she burrowed deeper under her thick comforter.

Valerie slipped on her shoes and pulled a coat over her shoulders. Then she opened the front door and brought Annabelle out to go potty.

It was cold, but it hadn't snowed yet.

Thanksgiving was less than two weeks away. Valerie had usually spent it with friends, or alone. A slow smile tilted her lips when she realized that she'd finally have someone to share the holiday with— her daughter. They could make a menu and go shopping and then prepare the meal together. Valerie's mind began to fill with all sorts of plans.

After Annabelle went potty, Valerie brought her back into the house and fed her, then turned on the coffee pot before heading back upstairs.

"Time to get up," Valerie said as she went to Hailey's bed.

Hailey groaned. "I hate school."

"*Hate* is a strong word."

"Are you really the principal?" she asked.

"Yes."

Another groan.

"If you don't get into trouble," Valerie said with a smile, "then you have nothing to worry about." She touched Hailey's shoulder gently. "Come on. It's time to get up and get ready."

Hailey finally pushed back the covers and got up.

Valerie flipped on the lamp next to her bed—and was surprised to find Hailey's clothes from the day before on the floor.

"You have a laundry hamper," Valerie said as she picked up the clothes and put them into the wicker basket near the door.

Hailey glanced over her shoulder but didn't respond. Instead, she started to look through her clothes in the closest. The closet had a built-in dresser, so she rummaged through that, too. The clothes were soon messed up, some of them falling onto the floor near Hailey's feet, though she made no move to pick them up.

"You need to be more careful," Valerie said, moving to stand beside her to fix the clothes. "You need to keep your clothes neatly folded."

Hailey looked up at her and frowned. "Why?"

"I like when things are organized," Valerie said, feeling like she needed to explain herself. "There are less chances for the clothes to get wrinkled and it's easier to see what your options are when they are folded neatly."

"I like when things are messy."

"No, you don't."

Hailey nodded. "I do. Ask Mom. She complained about it all the time."

At the mention of Valerie's mother, she tensed. They hadn't spoken since her mom had dropped Hailey off on Saturday—and Valerie wasn't sure if her mom would even call. Had she just abandoned them? Valerie was an adult and could deal with the ramifications—but could Hailey?

"Come on," Valerie said. "Get changed, brush your teeth, and comb your hair. I'll get dressed and then make a quick breakfast. We can't be late."

Thirty minutes later, Valerie was sipping her coffee and toasting a bagel for Hailey. It was just after six and she had called for

Hailey twice already. Valerie went to the bottom of the steps a third time. "We need to leave. Hurry!"

"Coming," Hailey said.

When Hailey finally joined her in the kitchen a few minutes later, Annabelle was by her feet. Hailey's hair was still uncombed, and her shirt was wrinkly.

She looked like she'd gone back to bed.

"Were you sleeping?" Valerie asked.

Hailey climbed onto the counter stool and shrugged sheepishly. "I accidentally fell back to sleep."

"You can't fall back to sleep after I wake you up. You need to follow my directions to the letter. Do you understand?"

Frowning, Hailey shook her head. "What does *to the letter* mean?"

"It means, you need to do as I say, when I say it and how I say it. I run a very tight schedule, and we can't be late. A lot of people depend on me."

"Mom let me sleep until right before we

left the house for school," she said. "She didn't make me do the letter thing."

"Well, Mom was irresponsible." Valerie's words slipped out before she could stop them. She recalled her mother's lackadaisical attitude when Valerie was a kid. They were late to everything—and she hated it. It was embarrassing to run into the classroom after the final bell when everyone else was in their seats. Or show up to the school field trip, only to see the bus pulling out of the parking lot without her. Her teachers were always scolding her—but it was rarely her fault. She refused to let Hailey experience the same humiliation.

"I want to go home," Hailey said, lowering her head to her arms, which were resting on the counter. Her shoulders began to shake as she cried.

Remorse filled Valerie as she set her coffee cup down and walked to Hailey's side. "I'm sorry, Hailey." She sighed. "Mom and I are two very different people. It'll take some time for you and me to get used to each other. But I have to be punctual and enforce the rules—it's how I do my job well."

The clock said six fifteen. Since Valerie only lived five blocks from the school, it wouldn't take her long to get there, but Hailey hadn't eaten breakfast yet.

"Come on," she said, not wanting to rush Hailey, but needing her to eat something. "I made you a bagel."

"I don't like bagels," she said as she wiped her cheeks.

"You told me yesterday you liked them when we bought them." Valerie tried not to feel impatient. "What would you like for breakfast?"

"Pancakes."

"I don't have time to make you pancakes this morning. I'll have to make them another day. We have the cereal you picked out yesterday."

Hailey lifted a shoulder.

Valerie didn't have time to debate with

her, or lecture her about wasting food, either. She went to the pantry and pulled out the cereal Hailey had chosen at the store. Her kitchen was neat and orderly, like the rest of her life—at least, like it used to be. She pulled out a bowl and dumped in some cereal, then added milk. She put it in front of Hailey with a spoon and said, "We need to be in the car in ten minutes. You should hurry."

Hailey took a few small bites of her cereal as Valerie grabbed their coats and bags. Thankfully, Hailey had a backpack among her suitcases, so Valerie didn't need to buy her a new one. Inside were all the school supplies she'd need. Her mother might not be punctual, but at least she'd been organized when she packed Hailey's things.

Valerie slipped on her wool coat and put Annabelle in her crate. Then she went back to the kitchen and discovered that Hailey had barely touched her cereal.

"You're going to be hungry until lunch,"

Valerie warned. "But we don't have any more time." She handed Hailey her coat, hating that she wouldn't have time to clean up the cereal bowl until after school. "Grab an apple or a banana, and let's go."

Hailey took her time putting on her coat—and Valerie realized her hair was still uncombed. She couldn't have her daughter show up to her first day of school without her hair combed.

"Just a second," Valerie said as she ran out of the kitchen, up the stairs, and into the bathroom to grab a comb. Her heart was pounding as she ran back downstairs and into the kitchen. "Comb it as we drive."

She ushered Hailey out, realizing she had not finished her coffee, but couldn't do anything about it. They were late.

The air was cold as they ran from the house to the garage. She had to prod Hailey along, since the girl didn't seem too concerned about being late.

"Come on," Valerie said, her frustration mounting. "We need to hurry."

Valerie hated feeling stressed and unraveled. She also hated losing her cool around children. As an adult, she was an example. But Hailey was testing her patience.

A few minutes later, she pulled into the parking lot and found Wade Griffin's truck already there. She was late—again.

"I don't want Issy to know you're my mom," Hailey said as Valerie turned off the car.

"She's going to find out, Hailey." Valerie pivoted in her seat to look at her daughter.

"Why?"

"Because I have to tell my staff the truth—and this kind of thing doesn't stay quiet for long."

Tears rimmed Hailey's eyelids. "I don't want anyone to know."

Pain sliced through Valerie. Was Hailey embarrassed by her? Was that why she didn't want people to know? "Why?"

"Because you're not my mom. I have a mom."

Valerie tried not to take it personally, but it was impossible. "I am your biological mother—"

"You're not my mom."

"Hailey—"

"Please don't tell anyone."

Valerie stared at Hailey, knowing that Wade was waiting for her to open the school. How was she going to navigate this tricky situation? Hailey had been dealing with so much trauma, would it be helpful to keep everything a secret a little longer? Give her time to figure things out? As the principal, she was the only person who needed to know the truth. The rest of the staff could be told that Hailey was her sister. It didn't really matter, as long as they knew she was Hailey's legal guardian. She didn't want to keep the truth from everyone—but in Hailey's eyes, Valerie wasn't her mom.

"I'll try to keep it quiet," Valerie said.

Hailey nodded as she wiped her tears for the second time that morning.

"But we can't keep it a secret forever."

Hailey caught sight of Issy, who had gotten out of her dad's truck. Hailey opened the door and left Valerie's car without another word.

Wade was leaning against his truck, waiting for Valerie.

She felt awful that she was late again— and that she had agreed to keep Hailey's parentage a secret.

"Sorry," Valerie said as she got out of her car, feeling rattled and unsettled again. "I promise I'm not usually late."

He grinned and she couldn't help but return his smile. He had been a bright spot over the past weekend—the only one she'd had.

"No need to apologize," he said. "It'll take some time for you two to figure things out."

"Thank you for understanding." She pulled her keys from her shoulder bag.

"You don't know how much that means to me."

She'd never noticed how blue his eyes were or how his mouth tilted at a charming angle when he smiled. He wore a beard, trimmed close, and his brown hair was a little longer, curling at the ends. He was a head taller than her and he was muscular and fit, probably from all his construction work.

There was a lot she hadn't noticed about Wade Griffin—but she had given up on a happily-ever-after when Soren had abandoned her in high school. She wasn't about to put herself in a position to be wounded again. It was easier to keep men at arm's length and not let them get close enough to hurt or use her.

No matter how cute or understanding Wade Griffin might be, it was best if she kept him at a distance, too.

For some reason, Wade couldn't get Valerie Wilmington out of his head all that morning. He should have been focused on the construction project, but his thoughts returned to her every chance they could get. She'd been just as flustered this morning as she had been Saturday and he kind of liked it. There was something attractive about being real and vulnerable, especially from a woman who seemed to pride herself on always having her life together.

She was also really pretty, which didn't hurt.

"How's it going in here?" A feminine voice broke into his thoughts. The voice of the woman he'd been thinking about— again.

He turned from where he was tearing out the wet Sheetrock and smiled at Valerie.

She was wearing a long black skirt and a simple white blouse today. Her hair was up in a twist at the back, and she had on a pair of glasses, though she didn't wear them all the time.

Wade's crew was hard at work tearing

out the rest of the Sheetrock and the ruined cabinets.

"It's going well." He put the ruined Sheetrock into a bin to be hauled away and approached her.

"The lunch bell is going to ring soon," she said. "I wanted to let you and your crew know that you're welcome to have lunch on us today."

"Thank you." Wade glanced at his men, who were nodding their appreciation.

"You can head into the cafeteria at 12:05," she said, glancing at the watch on her wrist.

"12:05?" He smiled. "Exactly?"

"The school day is run on a tight schedule," she said, not realizing he was teasing her. "The kids go in at twenty-minute intervals, starting at eleven twenty. All the grades should be through by twelve and your men can go behind them."

"*We* won't be late," he teased her again, wondering if she'd respond.

She did—smiling at him. "Unlike some people?"

"I won't name any names."

"Good. I have a reputation to uphold."

They were still smiling at each other. Then she quickly looked away, inspecting the room. "You've made great progress here. Any idea how long this will take?"

He was happy she was changing the subject. He was tempted to keep teasing her, to see if he could get her to show her dimples or laugh again. He still remembered the charming sound and how it had made him feel.

But it was best if he didn't think about her laugh or her dimples—or her in general. It was better to think about the construction project.

"I'm hoping that we can finish the demolition work today and start hanging new drywall tomorrow. It'll take a couple of days to get the mudding and taping done and then another day to spray the walls. Then we'll paint them. Early next week, we'll lay the carpet and install the new cabinets."

"Does that mean the kids will be back in here after Thanksgiving break?"

"Yes—I feel confident we can get them in here by then."

"Thank you." She sighed. "That's such a relief. I'd love if it could be before Thanksgiving, but I'll take what I can get."

A man entered the room and Wade's shoulders tightened. It was his father.

"Hey, Dad," Wade said, wondering what his father had come to critique this time.

Wade had gone to college to learn music composition. He had dreamed of being a singer–songwriter. But life had taken a different course. When he and Amber found out Isabel was on the way during their senior year of college, they had gotten married and then he had needed a real job. But there was little available to a man with a degree in music composition, so he'd taken a job at a home-improvement store, finishing his degree and working on his music on the weekends. Then, Brayden had come along—and a year later, Amber had left.

The Twin Cities had been hectic and expensive, so when his dad had offered him a job with the family construction business back in his hometown, he'd had little choice. It was the last thing he wanted to do—but he'd settled into life in Timber Falls faster than expected.

Sometimes, at night, he still pulled his guitar out—but he was usually too tired to be creative. And the grief that had come with the loss of his dreams had weighed heavier on him than he sometimes realized.

"This is Miss Wilmington," Wade said to his father.

"I know," his dad said as he smiled at Valerie. "We met at church."

"It's nice to see you again, Mr. Griffin," Valerie said.

"You can call me Fred," his dad responded. "And we're happy you called on Griffin Construction for this project." His dad was a good salesperson. He was charming when he wanted to be—harsh when he liked to be. Usually toward Wade who didn't seem to live up to his expectations.

"Of course," Valerie said. "We like to utilize the businesses of our school families whenever we can."

"Well, we appreciate it." His dad looked around the room, and his smile fell into a frown. "I thought the crew would be further along by now. What's the holdup, Wade?"

Embarrassment warmed Wade's neck. "I think we're making great progress."

His dad shook his head, offering Valerie a long-suffering look. "It's a good thing I showed up when I did. I'll get these guys whipped into shape, yet."

Valerie smiled politely, but the air had grown tense and awkward.

"Come on," his dad said to Wade. "Stop flirting with this pretty lady and get some work done. I'm not paying you to stand around all day and work on your love life."

"Dad." Wade gave his dad a look.

"I'll leave you to it," Valerie said, her cheeks turning pink.

Wade didn't even know what to say as she walked out of the classroom.

"Come on," Wade said to his dad. "That wasn't necessary. You embarrassed her."

"It looks like I embarrassed you, too," he said, though he wasn't smiling. "Which means I hit close to home. You *were* flirting with her."

"She's Issy and Brayden's principal. I was being nice."

"Sure," his dad said, though he didn't sound convinced. "We can't afford to stay on this project for long. There's no time for being *nice* to anyone."

Wade had learned a long time ago that it didn't pay to argue with his dad.

He would apologize to Valerie later— but for now, he needed to get the job done.

Though the sooner he got it done, the

sooner he wouldn't have an excuse to see her.

And that thought made him more disappointed than it should.

Chapter Four

Valerie watched as the last bus left the parking lot at the end of the school day. The temperature had dropped, and the forecast said there was snow on the way. A heavy gray sky overhead and a biting wind were all the evidence she needed as she blew into her hands and reentered the building. She was eager to get back into her office where she'd told Hailey to wait after the last bell. Mrs. Freeman, the school secretary, had agreed to keep her eye on the little girl until Valerie was done with bus duty, and Valerie was thankful. She had worried about her daughter far more than she expected.

It was strange having Hailey in the school. All day long, Valerie's thoughts had strayed to her daughter. Was she getting along with her classmates? Did she like her teacher? Was she where she needed to be academically? Valerie had wanted to check on her in the fifth-grade classroom several times that morning and afternoon but had forced herself to keep her distance.

How did parents do this every day? She'd only been responsible for Hailey for three days and she was a mess worrying about her. Thankfully, she'd gotten a glimpse of her during lunch and saw that Hailey was grinning with Issy and a couple of other girls she had befriended. She'd hardly paid attention to Valerie, which caused a new worry. Was Hailey ignoring her? Pretending like she didn't know her? Embarrassed to be related to the principal?

Noise from the kindergarten classroom drew Valerie's attention as she walked closer to the office. Wade and his crew would work until five. Mrs. Freeman had volunteered to stay to lock up the building, since Valerie didn't want to make Hailey wait around longer than necessary.

As Valerie entered the office, she was surprised to find Issy sitting with Hailey in the waiting area.

"Hi," Valerie said to the girls. "Did you miss your bus, Issy?"

"Daddy said I could wait here until he's done," she said. "I don't like going to my day care after school. There is a baby who cries and cries all the time."

"Can Issy come home with us?" Hailey asked, her blue eyes wide as she begged. "Please?"

"I don't know, Hailey," Valerie said. "We're just trying to get used to every-thing, and—"

"Please," Hailey said. "She's my new best friend. I want to show her my friend-ship bracelet collection. She's never made a friendship bracelet and I want to show her how."

Valerie couldn't think of a good reason to say no. They were still getting used to each other, but wasn't this part of the process? Letting Hailey make friends and feel like she was at home in Timber Falls? That Valerie's house was Hailey's house, too?

"Okay," Valerie finally said.

The girls started to cheer, so Valerie put up her hand. "I still need to ask Issy's dad."

"Come on," Hailey said to Issy. "Let's go ask."

"*I* need to ask," Valerie said as she followed the girls out of her office.

The girls didn't seem to hear her as they giggled and walked hand in hand down the hall.

"Wait for me," Valerie said, a little louder and harsher than she intended. "I don't know if it's safe to go into the kindergarten room."

Hailey stopped and frowned. "Why wouldn't it be safe?"

"Construction zones are usually dangerous," Valerie explained as she caught up to them, bringing her voice back to a reasonable level. "There could be large equipment or building material that could fall on you."

The look of concern on Hailey's and Issy's faces made Valerie realize she needed to speak a little calmer and more rationally. "It's always best to wait until you know it's safe to enter a construction zone."

The sound of electric drills and men's voices met Valerie's ears as she slowly opened the door to the room.

Wade was drilling a screw into a new piece of Sheetrock as another man was holding it in place. Two other guys were doing the same on a different piece.

When Wade saw Valerie and the girls, he grinned—and Valerie's heart filled with warmth at the greeting. "Hi," he said.

"Hi."

"Let me finish up here and I'll be with you in a second." He finished screwing the Sheetrock into place and then wiped his hands on his Carhartt pants as he approached. "I hope Issy isn't causing trouble." He touched his daughter's nose, making her giggle.

"Not at all."

"I told her she could come in here and wait for us to finish, if you needed to lock up the office."

"That's actually what I came to talk to you about—"

"Can I go to Hailey's house?" Issy asked her dad. "Miss Wilmington said it would be okay. You can pick me up when you're done working."

"And then you can stay for supper," Hailey said with a grin. "Valerie is making baked macaroni and cheese. I'm not sure it'll be as good as the boxed macaroni and cheese, but she thinks so."

Wade chuckled and Valerie smiled, but then Wade said to his daughter, "I don't know. I don't want to be an inconvenience to Miss Wilmington."

"It's not an inconvenience," Valerie said, though she wasn't so sure about the supper part. "Hailey is new to town and it's important to me that she makes good friends. Issy is a wonderful girl and I'd love if she came over for the afternoon to play with Hailey."

Wade studied Valerie for a second and then nodded. "If you don't mind."

"Of course not." She didn't want to be rude and overlook Hailey's invitation for them to come for supper. "And we'd love for you and Brayden to join us for supper. My baked macaroni and cheese might not be as good as the boxed stuff," she said with a cheeky smile, "but my recipe feeds several people. Hailey and I can't possibly eat it all."

His eyes were shining as he said, "My mother told me to never pass up an invitation for supper."

The girls squealed with delight and jumped up and down as they hugged.

Valerie returned his smile, glad that Hailey was happy. "Then it's settled. I'll have it ready by five thirty. Hopefully that gives you time to pick up Brayden after you get done here."

"That should be plenty of time. Can I bring something?"

"No. It's my treat."

"Perfect. Thanks." He paused and then said, "And I wanted to apologize for my dad earlier. Sometimes he says things that make people uncom—"

"Don't worry about it," she said, her cheeks warming at the memory. "I know construction sites have a reputation for—"

"Not my construction sites," he said. "Women should always be respected, no matter what kind of work environment it is. I don't like when people feel uncomfortable, so I'm sorry."

"You don't owe me an apology, but I'll accept it." She wondered about this man. She hadn't thought much about him in the past few months since coming to Timber Falls, but recently, it seemed their paths were crossing constantly, and he was a pleasant surprise. She loved the idea of his daughter becoming friends with hers. She'd learned early on in her education degree and working in schools that friends were the key to a student's future, whether good or bad. And she wanted to make sure Hailey's friends were kind, thoughtful and caring.

She gave him her phone number and her address. He said he knew the house, since he'd done some work on the bathroom a couple of years ago.

"I should get back to work," he said. "I'll see you soon."

"Bye, Daddy!" Issy said as she and Hailey ran out of the room.

"Bye," Valerie said as she left to join the girls.

How strange her life felt. Just a week ago, she wouldn't have imagined that she would have her daughter in her house. Now she would have two little girls— and then a handsome man and his son join them later. She hadn't entertained since she'd come to Timber Falls—and the last people she thought she'd invite over were a single dad and two of her students.

Yet that's where she found herself—and she was strangely excited about the prospect. She'd been alone for a long time and had convinced herself that she was okay with it. But the thought of having a full household filled her with inexplicable joy.

She returned to the office where the girls put on their coats and grabbed their backpacks.

Mrs. Freeman smiled at them from behind the front counter and then glanced up at Valerie. "It looks like they've become fast friends."

"It appears that way." Valerie grabbed her bag and coat, ready to take the girls home. She didn't share much with Mrs. Freeman, learning early on that the school secretary was also the school gossip. The first week Valerie was in Timber Falls, Mrs. Freeman had shared very personal details about each of the teachers' and parents' lives—claiming all of it was public knowledge, though Valerie had quickly learned otherwise. Eventually, Valerie had to ask her not to share any more. She didn't want to know—and was aware that if Mrs. Freeman was sharing personal details about other people's lives, she'd share them about Valerie's, too, if she had the chance.

"I'm staying for supper at Miss Wilmington's," Issy said. "And Daddy is coming, too."

Mrs. Freeman's eyebrows rose high on her forehead as she looked to Valerie for confirmation. "Is that so?"

Valerie didn't confirm or deny the statement. Instead, she said, "Have a good night, Mrs. Freeman. Thank you for staying late to lock up."

"My pleasure," she said, though Valerie could tell she was disappointed that she wouldn't tell her more.

Wade felt strangely nervous as he and Brayden pulled up to Valerie's house at five thirty. He knew it wasn't a date, but he also knew that he didn't have supper with single women who weren't related to him. He hadn't been on a date since he had dated his ex-wife. There hadn't even been anyone he was interested in dating after he was divorced. His world was his children and his work.

What if he and Valerie didn't have anything to talk about? What if it was awkward and uncomfortable? He remembered the early years of dating before he'd met Amber. He'd had some painful experiences he'd rather forget. Thankfully, he didn't have to face any of those women afterward. If this supper was weird and uncomfortable, he'd still have to see Valerie in his day-to-day life. Whether he was dropping his kids off at school or going to church on Sundays, she was unavoidable.

But this wasn't a date—so he didn't have to worry about it. That's what he kept telling himself as he and Brayden got out of his truck and walked up the front sidewalk to Valerie's house.

Soft snowflakes fell out of the heavy clouds overhead. It was dark and the lights were on in Valerie's house, offering a soft glow on the lawn. Wade had thought this was a beautiful home when he worked on the bathroom remodel a few years ago. He would have never imagined that he'd be coming back to have supper with such an intriguing and beautiful woman.

He tried to shake off the thought. Valerie Wilmington was his children's principal and nothing more. It didn't matter if he found her attractive. That wasn't what this meal was about.

"Can I ring the doorbell?" Brayden asked Wade.

"Go ahead, buddy."

Brayden grinned as he pressed the lighted button.

Wade's heart pounded hard when he heard the sound and knew that Valerie would be opening the door any second.

He tried to think about some topics they could discuss. The weather. The remodeling project at school—

All thoughts slipped from his mind when the door opened, and Valerie appeared.

She was wearing jeans and a simple button-down shirt, rolled at the sleeves. She had on a pair of slippers and her hair was in a braid.

She looked relaxed and welcoming as she smiled. "Hi, guys."

Wade's pulse ticked up a notch—but he had to remind himself this wasn't a date. This wasn't even really a social visit. If it wasn't for Issy and Hailey's friendship, she wouldn't have asked him to come.

"Hi," he managed to say.

"Come on in." She held the door open for them and stepped aside. "The girls are upstairs," she said to Brayden.

Brayden slipped off his shoes and handed his coat to Wade and then ran up the stairs.

Valerie laughed as she took the coat from Wade. "Let me hang that up for you."

He entered her house, surprised at how different it looked with someone else's furnishings.

Valerie had an elegant style that matched the house perfectly. It was warm and inviting, but also looked like it could be in a magazine. A soft light came from the lamps and the smell of baked macaroni and cheese mingled with a sweet scented candle glimmering in the living room.

"Your house is beautiful," he said.

"Thank you. I've enjoyed making it my own."

The sound of laughter filtered down from upstairs and Wade breathed a sigh of relief. "Sounds like the girls are okay with Brayden joining them. Issy's not always excited about her little brother tagging along."

Valerie took Wade's coat next and hung it up by Brayden's. "Issy is such a sweet girl. I can't imagine her not including him."

Wade laughed. "Don't let her deceive you. They get in their fair share of fights."

"I'm sure they do." She stood at the foot of the stairs, near the front door, smiling.

The moment drew on for a second too long and Wade started to panic, afraid it was about to get awkward.

"Can I help in the kitchen?" he asked quickly.

"The food is ready, but I could use some help setting the table."

"Great."

He followed her through the living room, into the dining room and then the kitchen.

Everything was neat and orderly—nothing like Wade's house, which often looked like a tornado had gone through it.

"How do you do it?"

"What?" she asked.

"Keep this place so tidy? My kids seem to enjoy making a mess."

Valerie opened a cupboard and took out a stack of plates. "You have to remember that until four days ago, I lived alone.

Since Hailey moved in with me, I've already talked to her three times about picking up after herself."

He wasn't sure if she'd tell him why Hailey had moved in so suddenly—but he was willing to try. "Can I ask how it is that she came to live with you?"

Valerie paused as she took out five glass cups from another cupboard. "It's a long story."

"I have all night."

She turned her back on him and began to take utensils out of a drawer—and Wade sensed she didn't want to talk about it after all.

"It's complicated," she said. "And Hailey doesn't want me telling people what happened. Maybe, when she's comfortable, she'll let me share it. But for now, I'd like to respect her privacy."

"I understand," he said, admiring her for honoring Hailey's wishes.

"Thanks." She stacked the utensils on

the plates and then handed them to him. "I'll grab some napkins."

Wade started to set the table and a couple minutes later, Valerie joined him, smiling as she laid out the napkins.

He didn't want the whole night to feel stilted and awkward—so he said the first thing that came to mind. "I think you're doing a great job at the school."

Her smile was bright, and her dimples shone. "Thank you."

"Really. It's a tough job, but the kids seem to respect you. That's not easy to do."

"I love working with them. For the most part, everyone has been really welcoming. They were great to Hailey today, too."

"I'm happy to hear that. I wasn't too excited about coming back to Timber Falls after my ex-wife left, but I'm thankful for the community and how they're helping me raise the kids."

"You haven't lived in Timber Falls your whole life?" Valerie asked.

"No. I left after high school and was

gone for about eight years. I went to school in Wisconsin. Those years away helped me better appreciate my hometown."

"Wisconsin?" She stopped putting the napkins on the table and stood up straight. "Where in Wisconsin?"

"La Crosse."

Her lips parted. "I went to the University of Wisconsin–La Crosse!"

"Really?" He frowned and then smiled. "When?"

"I started there ten years ago, right out of high school."

"You must have been a freshman in my senior year."

"What did you major in?"

"Music composition."

She shook her head and smiled. "That's amazing! Who would have thought that we have the same alma mater."

"That is incredible. Of all the colleges and universities in the country—we went to the same one."

They spent the rest of the evening chat-

ting about their university experiences
and even realized they had some friends
in common. Wade marveled that this one
thing had connected them in a way nothing else could and he chuckled to think he
was worried about what they would talk
about.

When it was time to call the kids down
to supper, they arrived with a small dog at
their heels. Hailey introduced him to Annabelle, and she licked him with enthusiasm as the kids washed up for supper.

Wade picked up the friendly dog as the
kids took turns at the kitchen sink and
Valerie pulled the baked macaroni and
cheese out of the oven. Her cheeks were
pink from the heat, and she smiled at the
kids as they chattered about the bracelets
they were making.

A funny pang hit Wade. It was a bittersweet feeling. He longed for this scene. For
a mom for his children. He did his best,
but he knew they were missing a feminine
touch in their lives—especially Issy. When

Amber had left, she'd taken that dream with him and he'd tried hard to not become bitter. But moments like this, when he saw what his little family was missing, he felt regrets start to pile up.

Soon, they were all seated at the dining room table. Annabelle sat next to Hailey on the ground, her nose lifted to the scents coming from the table. Wade was across from Valerie and the kids were spread out between them. The girls on one side and Brayden on the other.

"May I pray?" Valerie asked.

"Of course." Wade nodded, loving that she wanted to say grace.

His kids held out their hands from habit and Valerie seemed surprised. But she smiled and took Brayden's hand and then reached out and took Hailey's hand in the other.

Their two little families linked hands, and for a second, felt like one big family.

Valerie's gaze caught Wade's and the tenderness he saw there melted his heart.

If he wasn't careful, he might start to fall for Miss Valerie Wilmington and that was something he couldn't afford.

Chapter Five

Valerie hadn't laughed so much in years. Not only did Wade have a great sense of humor, but he was also a wonderful storyteller. She could sit and listen to him for hours.

"Tell the one about the mice, Daddy!" Issy said as her brown eyes lit up.

Wade laughed. "Why do you like that one so much?"

"Because it's funny!" Her laughter filled Valerie's dining room as Brayden started to giggle. Soon, Hailey and Valerie were laughing, too, though they hadn't even heard the story.

When their laughter had subsided, Wade told the story. "I was doing a remodeling job for an older couple, and they told me they had an antique light fixture in their back shed they wanted me to install."

"But when he opened the shed door, hundreds of mice ran out," Issy said, laughing so hard she almost fell off her seat, which made all of them laugh harder.

"There were several nests in the shed," Wade clarified, "and it wasn't hundreds—but definitely dozens of mice. The older couple was standing there, and they both grabbed shovels and tried to whack the mice as they ran in all directions. They didn't get a single one, but they sure looked funny trying."

"Daddy, show them how they looked," Issy said.

"No." He shook his head. "Not today."

"But that's the funniest part!" she said.

"Maybe another time."

"I'll show them!" Issy jumped off her

chair and began to dance around the dining room, causing more laughter.

Wade's smile was warm as he put his hand out to stop her and direct her back to her seat. He was so handsome, but what appealed to Valerie more was that he was both masculine and gentle. He treated his children with tenderness, though he was also disciplined and firm. Valerie could look at him all day—but she realized she was staring and turned her attention to the kids around the table. Their laughter was the thing missing from her home all these years and she hated to see the evening come to an end.

"Okay, kiddos," Wade said, "time to clear the table and fill the dishwasher. Miss Wilmington made supper. She shouldn't need to clean it up, too."

All three kids got up from the table and immediately began to clear the dishes—even taking Valerie's.

"Wow," Valerie said, "I could use your special touch in the school."

He shrugged, and then said, "It was a great meal. Thank you."

"You're welcome." She wasn't quite ready to say goodbye, so she said, "I have a question. It's about a project I've been thinking about."

"Oh?" He leaned forward, resting his arms on the tabletop. "What kind of project?"

"It's outside. I'm not sure there will be enough time left this season to work on it, but I'd like your opinion."

"I can take a look at it now."

"Okay."

They went into the living room to grab their coats from the hooks by the front door. After they were ready, she led him back into the dining room where Brayden was taking the cups off the table and then they went into the kitchen where the girls were filling the dishwasher.

"Wow," she said to them. "You guys look like you know what you're doing."

"We do," Issy said as she grinned.

"We're going to step outside for a minute," Valerie told them. "Leave the big dishes for me to hand-wash, okay?"

"You got it," Hailey said.

Valerie flipped on the backyard lights and then opened the door. Wade followed her outside.

The air was cold, and the snow was gathering on the ground, falling lazily from the sky. It was silent as it came to rest on the grass and the branches of the bare trees.

"I hadn't really thought about fixing it up before Hailey moved in," Valerie said as she walked across the yard and pointed at a large maple tree in the back corner. "But I'd love to know if it's possible."

A tree house sat in the branches and looked like it hadn't been used in over a decade.

"That's an impressive tree house," Wade said as he walked under the tree and looked up toward the structure. He was wearing a stocking cap and had his hands in his pockets for warmth. A cloud escaped his lips as he breathed the cold air.

Valerie had the opportunity to admire him as he gazed at the tree house.

It surprised her that he had a degree in music composition. She'd assumed that he had gone to school for carpentry work—or perhaps hadn't gone to college at all. Why hadn't he pursued a job in his degree? Was it because of his kids? There was so much about Wade Griffin that made Valerie curious, and the more time she spent with him, the more he surprised her.

"What are you thinking?" he asked as he turned his gaze back to her.

Her lips parted and heat warmed her cheeks—did he want to know what she was thinking about him? She could never tell him.

"What would you like to do with the tree house?" he clarified.

She let out a relieved breath and chuckled to herself. "First, I'd like to know if it's safe and stable enough for Hailey to use and, if it is, I'd like to fix it up. Maybe put on a new roof and repair any rotten boards. Things like that. How long do you think it would take?"

"A good couple of days," he said as he joined her again. "I could get it done in a weekend."

"Really?"

He shrugged. "Sure."

"Is it too late in the season to work on it?"

Wade shook his head. "No. It might be a little cold, but I work outside most of the year, so I'm used to it."

She wrapped her arms around herself for heat and asked, "Would you have time to get it done soon?"

He took a second to think and then nodded. "I could probably work on it this weekend."

"That soon?"

"If you'd like."

"I'd love that."

"Great." He smiled. "I can be here on Saturday morning."

"Wonderful." She motioned toward the house. "Let's get back inside and into the warmth."

They returned to the kitchen and found the kids still hard at work cleaning up supper.

"What were you doing out there?" Hailey asked them.

"Mr. Griffin is going to come over this weekend and work on the tree house for us," Valerie said.

Hailey's eyes opened wide. "Can Issy have a sleepover this weekend?"

Wade and Valerie looked at each other and Valerie started to shake her head. "I'm not sure about sleepovers, yet."

"Please," Hailey begged. "Mom let me have sleepovers all the time before I came here."

"We can talk about it later," Valerie told her.

"But I want her to sleep over."

"Hailey." Valerie wasn't used to children talking back to her or disobeying her orders. As a principal, children generally respected her wishes and rarely pushed back. Hailey seemed to push back almost every decision Valerie made.

Wade offered Valerie an understanding smile and said, "I'll plan to be here on Saturday morning around eight."

"Can Issy at least come over when her dad comes?" Hailey asked, dejected—and yet hopeful.

"Of course. Both Issy and Brayden are welcome to come over while their dad is here."

The girls cheered and Brayden got down on the floor with Annabelle and said, "Did you hear that, girl? I'm coming back to play with you on Saturday."

Wade took off his coat and put it on the kitchen stool and began to roll up his sleeves. "I'll help with those dishes before we head home."

"It's not necessary," Valerie protested.

"I insist." He went to the sink and began to fill it with warm, soapy water. "You made supper. The least I can do is clean the dishes."

She smiled. "As long as you let me help."

"I'd love your help." He returned her smile.

The kids ran off to keep playing while Valerie stepped up to the sink next to Wade and began to rinse and dry the dishes he washed.

They worked in companionable silence for a couple minutes, catching each other's gaze from time to time and smiling.

"Do the kids get to see their mom very often?" she asked.

He was quiet for a moment, and she regretted that she'd asked him a personal question. She hadn't been forthcoming when he asked her about Hailey—what made her think he'd want to talk about his ex-wife?

"They haven't seen her since she left. I

send her pictures, and she sends gifts for their birthdays and Christmas, but she's not part of our lives."

She heard the disappointment and pain in his voice, so she said, "I'm sorry."

He let out a breath. "I'm sorry, too, but I think it might be best this way. Amber didn't want to be a mom. We found out she was pregnant during our senior year of college. Both of us were able to graduate, but we had to work hard to make ends meet. Amber was a theater major, and she wanted to pursue a career on stage or film. We found ourselves barely hanging on when Issy was born. Then, Brayden came along, and it was too much for her. She went to California to try to break into the movies and I came back to Timber Falls to raise our children."

His story was similar to hers, in that they both had to deal with unexpected pregnancies. She wanted to share her experience, to let him know she understood—but she didn't want to betray Hailey's trust. Especially this early into their relationship.

"The children miss her," Wade continued, "but I've tried to explain it as best as I can. I don't hide anything from them. When they have tough questions, I don't shy away from the difficult answers. I believe the truth is always the best approach—no matter what the situation. It might be hard and painful, but keeping things hidden never works. Amber hid things from me all the time and it destroyed me."

His words hit her right in the gut, and she held her breath. She opened her mouth to tell Wade the truth about Hailey—but the words caught in her throat. She didn't owe Wade an explanation about her daughter or her situation. It was between her and Hailey. As soon as Hailey was ready to tell the truth, she would tell the world that she was her daughter.

Until then, she'd hold the truth close. It wasn't the same as lying—was it?

* * *

Wade was still smiling an hour after he left Valerie's house as he helped Issy and Brayden get ready for bed. The evening spent with the Wilmingtons had been good for all three of them. Wade hadn't smiled so much in so long, his cheeks hurt. Issy hadn't stopped talking about Hailey or the bracelets they'd made. And Brayden told Wade about all the tricks Annabelle could do. The little boy had wanted a dog for so long, the time spent with the small poodle had filled the empty place inside him. At least for a short while. No doubt he'd be bugging Wade for a dog again soon.

"Daddy," Issy said as he walked into her room at bedtime, "can we pray for Hailey and Miss Wilmington tonight?"

"Of course we can," he said as he pulled back her princess bedspread and she climbed in. "We can pray for anyone we want, any time we want."

"Not just for our family?" she asked.

"Prayers aren't reserved for just family." He chuckled. "Is that what you thought?"

She nodded as she pulled the covers up to her chin.

He moved her hair—damp from her bath—off her forehead and smiled at her. "God likes to hear about all the people we care about—and sometimes, even the people we don't care about. All of them are part of His family."

Her brown eyes were contemplative as she squinted. "Do you love Mommy?"

The question caught him off guard as he sat on the bed next to her, but he recalled the conversation he'd had with Valerie earlier. He didn't shy away from the tough questions. "What makes you ask that?"

"You always tell me to pray for her, but you don't have a nice face when you talk about her, so I thought maybe she's one of the people you don't like that we pray for."

Wade took a deep breath and clasped his

daughter's hands in his own. "Yes, I love your mommy. Not in the same way I used to, but she will forever be a part of my life, because she is your mommy. That makes me care about her."

"What about Miss Wilmington?" Issy asked next, searching his face. "Do you care about her?"

He shook his head at his little match-maker. "I don't know Miss Wilmington very well, but I care about her because she's your principal and that makes her important in your life. Anything that's important to you is important to me."

"She's very pretty."

"Isabel Marie Griffin," he said in a teasing voice that also had a hint of warning, "I know where you're going with this."

"What?" Issy asked. "Don't you want another wife?"

"Right now, I'm happy just being a dad." Even as he said the words, he knew they weren't completely true. He missed the companionship of a wife. Someone to share both the highs and lows of life. The responsibilities and the privileges. And the intimacy and connection.

"I want a mommy," she said, playing with the edge of her bedspread, her voice sad.

Wade's heart broke as he placed one hand on Issy's cheek. "I'm sorry you don't have a mommy, Issy. If I could change that for you, I would. But you have Grammy and lots of ladies at school and church who love you."

"But you *can* change that for me." She looked up, excitement in her eyes. "Miss Wilmington doesn't have a husband. I know. I asked Hailey. And now that Hailey is living with her, I could have a mommy and a sister."

"It's not that easy, Bug," he said with a sigh.

"Can you at least try?" she asked. "For me?"

He shook his head again. "You need to say your prayers and go to sleep."

"Okay. But I'm going to pray for Miss

Wilmington that she can become my mommy."

He wanted to groan, but he wasn't about to tell his daughter what she should pray for. He just hoped she wouldn't tell Valerie what she was doing.

After Issy's prayers and then Brayden's in the next room, Wade walked down the hall to the kitchen.

His home was a main level with a walk-out basement that faced the Mississippi River. There were three bedrooms on the main floor and two in the basement with a family room. Someday, when the kids were older, he might let them move into the basement, but for now, he liked having them on the main level where he slept.

The house was quiet as he walked to the large picture window looking out at his backyard and the river. Snow was starting to pile up. It clung to the tree branches and covered the deck and grass. He stood for a long time and just looked outside, his thoughts going in several different directions, but always coming back to Valerie Wilmington.

He couldn't lie to himself and say that he didn't find her attractive. But he also knew that he couldn't let himself fall for her. It had taken years for him to heal the broken pieces that Amber had left behind, and he wasn't sure he could do it again.

On nights like this one, when his spirit was unsettled, he itched to play his guitar and get lost in the melodies. But it had been a while since he'd taken his instrument out of the case.

Maybe it was time.

He went into the basement where he kept his guitar and gingerly removed it from the case. It took a couple of minutes to tune the strings and then he ran his fingers over them, closing his eyes at the sound.

He had written several songs in high school and college and played a few from memory. Then he played some of the more popular songs and a few that they sang in church each Sunday.

As he played, his fingertips began to ache, but his heart felt light for the first time in months.

This is where he belonged. This is what his soul yearned for. He needed to make music, to fill his heart with the melodies of songs that inspired him.

If only he could have found a way to have both his music and an income to provide for his family.

But regret wasn't healthy and after the last chord was played, he returned the guitar to its case and closed it.

Just like everything else, there was a time and a place for dreams. And his had come and gone.

Maybe someday, when his kids were grown, he'd find a way to make music again. For now, he was thankful for a steady job, healthy kids and new friendships.

As he climbed into bed later, he felt excited to wake up and go to work for the first time in a long time and he knew why.

He'd get to see Valerie at the school again.

He closed his eyes with a smile on his face, as new dreams began to fill his sleep.

Chapter Six

Valerie woke up the following Saturday with a smile on her face. The previous week had been difficult as she and Hailey had adjusted to a new normal. Each morning, Valerie had to prod Hailey out of bed to get dressed and eat something before school. But, as the week progressed, things started to get easier. Hailey had realized Valerie was serious about being prompt and by Friday morning, she had been at the kitchen island eating breakfast on time.

But today was Saturday and Valerie told Hailey she could sleep in a little later than usual.

It gave Valerie time to get in a workout, which she did in the living room with a video instructor. Then, after showering and getting dressed, she tapped lightly on Hailey's open door.

"Issy is going to be here in less than an hour," Valerie told her daughter.

Hailey sat up, a grin on her face, though she hadn't opened her eyes. "I haven't forgotten. We have a whole bunch of things planned today."

Annabelle was in bed with Hailey, even though she'd been up with Valerie earlier and had already gone out to go potty and had her breakfast.

"You should get dressed and eat breakfast before she comes," Valerie said as she entered Hailey's room.

Hailey yawned and slouched, resting a hand on Annabelle. "I will."

Valerie took a seat on Hailey's bed and moved the hair out of Hailey's face. In the past week, Valerie had gotten used to the idea of Hailey living with her. It was still a big adjustment, but the initial shock had worn off. She still hadn't told anyone the truth about Hailey, though it had almost slipped out several times.

Hailey let Valerie move the hair from her face, but she hadn't warmed up to Valerie, and quickly pulled away from her touch. She didn't give her hugs or ask to snuggle when they watched a movie together. She didn't sit close to Valerie, like she did Valerie's mom, or hold her hand, or show any affection. Valerie understood her reluctance and hadn't pushed her, but wanted her to know that Valerie was available, if she needed a hug.

"I think we need to talk about when we're going to tell people the truth about us," Valerie said. "It's going to come out eventually and we don't want people to think we lied to them."

Valerie had thought a lot about her conversation with Wade at the kitchen sink earlier that week. They'd seen each other many times since then, but they hadn't had a chance to share a serious conversation. She didn't want Wade to think she'd lied to him about Hailey. She knew how much he valued the truth—and though they hardly knew one another, she wanted him to trust her.

Hailey blinked her eyes open and shook her head. "I don't want anyone to know."

"Why?" Valerie tried not to feel hurt; after all, she had knowingly walked away from her daughter ten years ago. "Are you embarrassed by me? Because I'm the principal?"

"No." Hailey frowned.

"Then what is it?"

"I have a mom," she blurted out. "You're my sister. Why does that have to change?"

"Because it's not the truth."

"Yes, it is. You're not my mom. You've never been my mom."

Valerie let out a sigh. "I know, Hailey. For ten years, you had a different mom. But things have changed and now I am your mom."

"Not forever."

Valerie frowned. "What do you mean?"

"She'll come back and get me," Hailey said, her voice desperate. "She'll realize she misses me, and she'll come back. Then I'll go home with her, and you'll be my sister again."

Several seconds passed as Valerie tried to rein in her frustration with her mom for leaving Hailey on her doorstep when none of them were prepared—and frustration at herself for abandoning Hailey when she was just an infant.

"Mom and I made a big mistake," Valerie said, as calmly as she could. "But we're trying to make it right. Mom isn't coming back, Hailey. She got married and she's living in Arizona now. You are going to live here until you leave for college one day—and that's eight years from now. Sometime in those eight years, we need to tell people the truth. The sooner we do it, the less trouble we'll have. You don't want to keep the truth from Issy, do you?"

Hailey glared at Valerie. "I already told her that you're my sister and my mom left me here. She knows the truth."

Valerie briefly closed her eyes. If Hailey wasn't ready to tell people, then she wasn't in a place to say anything. For all intents and purposes, she wasn't Hailey's mom—at least, not yet. She hadn't earned that right.

"Okay," she told her daughter. "For now, we won't tell anyone. But, Hailey, when I feel the time is right, I will tell the truth. Do you understand? If it's necessary, I will tell people I'm your mom."

The little girl didn't speak as she continued to glare at Valerie.

"Come on," Valerie said with another sigh as she scooped Annabelle off the bed and put her on the wood floor. "You need to get up and get dressed. The Griffins will be here soon." She started to walk out of the room, but added, "And don't forget to make your bed."

Valerie left Hailey's bedroom and went downstairs to get breakfast ready, her heart heavy after their conversation. Hailey was the one suffering the most right now and she didn't want to push her faster or harder than necessary. But she also didn't like keeping the truth from people, either. Especially from Wade.

The timer was going off in the kitchen when Valerie entered. She had put together an egg bake the night before with spinach, bacon and Gruyère cheese, and had placed it in the oven when she had woken up earlier that morning. The delicious aroma coming from the kitchen made her mouth water as she turned off the timer, opened the oven and removed the egg bake.

It would need to sit for a while to set up, but Hailey probably wouldn't be down for another thirty minutes. It gave Valerie time to make a pot of coffee and spend some time praying.

The snow from last week had stayed, but it was just enough to give everything a little coating. Another storm was moving in, promising several more inches of accumulation. Valerie stood at her kitchen window with a cup of coffee and stared at her backyard where the tree house sat.

Her thoughts and prayers eventually strayed to Wade, as they had all week. Each time she saw him, her desire to see him again grew stronger. And that wasn't something she could deal with right now. Not with becoming a new mom and trying to get settled in a new town. Wade Griffin was a complication she didn't have time for.

So then why was she so excited about spending the day with him?

Forty-five minutes later, she and Hailey were just wrapping up breakfast when the front doorbell rang.

"I'll get it!" Hailey yelled as she ran toward the front door. She had appeared to have forgotten their tough conversation earlier and had come downstairs in a happier mood. Now, she was thrilled at the Griffin family's arrival.

"Hi!" Hailey said as she opened the door and practically pulled Issy inside. "We don't have any time to lose!"

Wade and Brayden stood behind Issy and seemed just as surprised as Issy at Hailey's excited greeting.

When Brayden saw Annabelle running toward him, he fell to the ground and began to play with the dog, letting her lick his face, laughing hysterically.

Wade smiled at Valerie, and she smiled back.

"I feel like we should be greeting each other with the same kind of enthusiasm as the kids and Annabelle," Wade said with a chuckle.

Valerie laughed and shook her head. "It's tempting—but you might turn and run if I greeted you that way."

His smile transformed into a grin. "You never know."

Her cheeks grew warm at the thought of throwing herself into his arms, so she ignored his teasing—or was it flirting?—and motioned for them to come in off the cold front porch.

"I'm going to get right to work," Wade said to Valerie. "Holler at me if you need anything."

"Okay—and come in when you get cold. I think the kids and I will do some baking today. I'll have lunch ready at noon."

"Great." Wade smiled again—and Valerie had to remind herself she wasn't thinking about him in a romantic way. He was a friend—nothing more. She would keep him at a distance.

She had a feeling that she would need to remind herself of that many times throughout the day.

Wade rarely whistled when he worked—and never when he was outside on a cold, windy day. But there was something different about working on a project for a woman he admired and a child who needed something good in her life. He'd been happy to discover that the tree house structure was better than he'd anticipated. The floor and walls were sturdy and though the roof needed new shingles, there hadn't been any damage done to the building from leaks. An old beehive had taken up residence, but Wade had gotten rid of it right away and with a little bit of cleaning and a few new boards here and there, the tree house would be ready to use.

He was on the roof of the tree house, putting on new shingles, but his gaze landed on Valerie's home every few minutes. He'd rather be inside with her and the kids than out on the tree house roof—but it gave him time to think. And he liked to think.

He'd asked Issy what she knew about Hailey's past, but all she knew was that Hailey's mom had gotten remarried and had sent Hailey to live with her older sister—Valerie. Apparently, her mother's new, rich husband didn't want kids at his house.

Wade couldn't imagine what Hailey—and Valerie—were going through. Hailey was probably feeling all kinds of abandonment and Valerie was probably resentful that her mother refused to raise her own daughter. No wonder Valerie hadn't wanted to talk about it. The whole situation painted Valerie's mom in a bad light. What kind of woman abandoned her ten-year-old daughter to run off and get remarried? Especially to a man who didn't want anything to do with her daughter?

Wade caught his thoughts. His wife had done that exact same thing—but Issy and Brayden had been a lot younger. Maybe that was why the girls had bonded so quickly. They understood what it felt like to be abandoned by their mothers.

The roof was about half done when Valerie came outside and shielded her hand against the sun to look up at him.

"How's it going?" she asked.

"Great! I should be able to wrap the roof up by supper time and finish up the rest tomorrow afternoon, after church."

"That is wonderful!" she said. "Lunch is ready. Are you hungry?"

"Starving. I'll be down in a minute."

She went back into the house and Wade climbed off the roof. It wasn't ideal to be on the roof after the first snowfall of the year, but the shingles had warmed up enough under the sun to melt the snow. He gingerly climbed down the ladder he'd placed on the tree house deck and then he climbed down the ladder that had been built on the trunk of the tree.

After picking up a few of his tools, he walked across the lawn and through the back door.

The house smelled like baked cookies and something savory—maybe turkey? Warmth and laughter met him at the door. The children were in the dining room, setting the table, while Valerie pulled something from the oven.

Annabelle greeted Wade at the door with her tail wagging happily.

It struck Wade, all over again, that this was what he wanted. This very scene, every time he walked into the house. It filled him with such joy and longing, it took his breath away.

And when Valerie saw him standing there, and she offered him a welcoming smile, it went straight to his heart.

"Come in and wash up," she said as she set a baking sheet on the island. "I made warm turkey-and-Gouda sandwiches for lunch. I hope you like them."

"They smell delicious." He closed the door and took off his boots. "You're going to spoil me and the kids. I'm not much of a cook. We eat a lot of frozen pizzas and Hamburger Helper."

"I love to cook. It relaxes me."

He lifted his eyebrows. "It's one of the more stressful parts of my day. Don't get me wrong, I love a good meal, but it's a never-ending chore."

She giggled, revealing her dimples. "I guess I don't look at it that way. To me, it's a never-ending opportunity to try something new."

"That's definitely a better perspective," he agreed as he went to the sink to wash his hands. "Maybe I should take lessons."

"I'm happy to share some recipes with you," she offered as she scooped the warm sandwiches off the baking sheet and onto a serving platter.

"You'd do that?"

"Of course." She shrugged. "One single parent to the next."

He quickly finished washing his hands and then helped her take the meal into the dining room where the kids were eagerly waiting.

After they prayed, everyone dug into the meal with enthusiasm. Along with the warm sandwiches, Valerie had made a pasta salad and served kettle chips and fresh fruit. There was also a heaping plate of chocolate chip cookies waiting for dessert.

"Are you kids having fun?" Wade asked the girls.

"Yes!" Issy said. "We've played dolls and painted pictures and made more bracelets and baked cookies!"

"That sounds like a lot of fun," Wade agreed.

"Can Hailey come to our house soon?" Issy asked him. "I want to show her my toys."

Wade glanced at Valerie and nodded. "I don't think that's a problem—do you?"

"I think that's a great idea," Valerie said.

"How about for Thanksgiving?" Issy asked, her brown eyes wide with excitement. "That's only five days away. My teacher told me so."

"Oh." Wade wasn't sure what to say as he met Valerie's gaze again. He couldn't be rude. "Of course. Yes, we'd be happy to have you and Hailey over for Thanksgiving supper—if you don't have plans already."

"We don't," Hailey said with a sigh. "It's just me and Valerie. No one else. My mom is living in Arizona with her new husband and hasn't even called us yet."

"Hailey," Valerie said in a reprimanding voice. "I don't think Mr. Griffin is interested in our family drama."

"But it's true," Hailey said.

Valerie smiled—though it was a tight smile and didn't reach her eyes. "We can talk about that later."

"We talk about an awful lot later," Hailey lamented.

"You don't need to give me an answer right away," Wade told Valerie quickly. The more he thought about it, though, the more he liked the idea of having her and Hailey over for Thanksgiving. "We go to my parents' in the morning and have brunch and then head home and do our own Thanksgiving meal together—just the kids and me."

"Hailey and I couldn't interrupt your tradition," she said.

"You wouldn't interrupt anything," he reassured her. "My parents have always gone to Thanksgiving bingo in the evening—it's a fundraiser for one of their charities, so it's not really by choice that we have a meal alone. We'd love to include more people."

Issy and Brayden nodded enthusiastically.

"And you can bring Annabelle," Brayden said with a grin.

Valerie looked uncertain, so Wade didn't want to pressure her.

"You and Hailey can talk it over," he said. "And you can let me know whenever it works for you."

"At church tomorrow," Hailey said. "When we sit together again."

"Yes," Issy agreed.

Wade found himself chuckling at his daughter and when he met Valerie's gaze, she was smiling, too.

"It looks like they're not giving us much of a chance to protest," he said.

"I'm sensing the same thing."

Wade wasn't unhappy about it. Maybe he'd even nudge Issy to nudge Hailey to talk to Valerie about coming for Thanksgiving.

It was the best idea his daughter had come up with so far.

Chapter Seven

The parking lot was full the next morning as Valerie pulled up to the church. She and Hailey had left the house on time and were both in good moods—something that hadn't happened often over the past week. Maybe it was due, in part, to the good time they'd had with Wade and his children yesterday. Hailey's friendship with Issy was growing and the girls had played happily for hours. Valerie's friendship with Wade was also growing and she hadn't realized, until now, how much she wanted more friendships.

"Can we sit with Issy's family again?"

Hailey asked as they got out of the car and walked toward the church.

"That's fine," Valerie said.

"And can we go to their house for Thanksgiving?"

Valerie let out a sigh. As much as she liked Wade, and enjoyed his friendship, she wasn't sure if going to his house for a holiday was a good idea. What might people think if they found out? Would they assume she and Wade were dating? Worse—what would Wade think? She suspected that he was attracted to her—and he probably noticed she was attracted to him—but she couldn't let it go any further. Spending a holiday together might give him the wrong idea.

Worse, it might give her heart the wrong idea.

"I don't think so," Valerie said. "We can—"

"Why?" Hailey asked, stopping in the middle of the cold parking lot.

Snow had fallen the night before, creating a winter wonderland in Timber Falls. It painted all the surfaces with crystal-white powder.

Valerie glanced around the parking lot. Thankfully there was no one within earshot. But she stepped closer to her daughter, just the same. "This isn't the place to talk about it."

"Why can't we go to their house?" she asked, her blue eyes wide with confusion. "I don't want to be alone."

"You won't be alone," Valerie said. "You'll be with me."

"Mom and I always had a big Thanksgiving meal with our friends. Why can't I be with my friend Issy?"

Valerie didn't always give in to Hailey—especially when it came to things that really mattered, like safety and health—but this wasn't one of those things. Was it? It was a simple holiday meal. People may talk, though that wasn't her problem. And she could be upfront with Wade if he showed any sign of romantic interest. They could keep things on a friendly basis.

They had to.

"I'll talk to Issy's dad," Valerie said to Hailey. "But I'm not making any promises."

"Yay!" Hailey ran toward the church doors and pulled one open for Valerie. "Can we bring pumpkin pie? I love pumpkin pie."

"I do too," Valerie said, surprised again by what she and her daughter had in common. "With whipped cream topping."

"Me too!"

They entered the church and Hailey ran off to find Issy and some of the other girls she'd become friends with the past week at school. Valerie saw her friend Liv Harris near the coffee bar and walked her way.

Liv was on the Timber Falls Christian School board and had been one of the people who had interviewed Valerie when she applied for the principal's job. They had hit it off immediately and Liv had been a good friend ever since.

"Hey, Valerie," Liv said as she turned

from the coffee bar and blew on the cup of coffee in her hand.

"Hey." Valerie smiled.

"How are things going with Hailey?" Liv asked, watching Valerie carefully. She was perceptive and a good listener. Valerie valued both those things.

Valerie let out a sigh and Liv put her hand on Valerie's arm. "That bad?" she asked.

"No. I'm just a little tired. I don't know how you do it with three children."

Liv smiled. Her oldest daughter, Miley, was almost thirteen and her second daughter, Alexis, was eight. Her youngest daughter, Natalie, was just two years old and was with Liv's husband, Zane, just a few feet away. "I've had some time to get used to being a mom," she said, though Valerie knew she hadn't been doing it for long. Liv had given birth to Miley when she was in high school. Liv had given up her rights to the little girl—never knowing that her boyfriend at the time, Zane, hadn't. He'd raised their daughter on his own and ten years later, their paths had crossed after he'd been married and then widowed. Alexis was his late wife's daughter. But as soon as he and Liv had married three years ago, Alexis had become her daughter, too.

"It'll take some time to get used to," Liv told Valerie. "I'm sure you never dreamed you'd become a mom to a ten-year-old girl."

Valerie shook her head—though there had always been a part of her that had wondered what it would be like. She hadn't expected her mom to drop Hailey off without warning—but it wasn't a complete surprise, either. After all, Hailey *was* her daughter.

"I had a lot to get used to when I married Zane," Liv continued, "though, I wasn't doing it alone. You need to give yourself some grace, Valerie."

Valerie tried to smile and nod. She wanted to tell Liv the truth—to tell someone—but could she trust Liv with the truth? She had a feeling Liv would understand, maybe more than most people. More importantly, Liv had proven to be trustworthy.

"There's more to the story," Valerie conceded as she glanced around to make sure no one was listening.

Liv took a step closer, curiosity in her gaze.

"I need to tell someone," Valerie said. "Hailey isn't my sister, as I've led people to believe." She lowered her voice. "She's my daughter. My mom has been raising her, but left her with me to get remarried."

Understanding radiated from Liv's kind eyes. "You must be feeling a lot of things right now. Can I ask why you haven't told people the truth?"

Valerie nibbled her bottom lip, both happy she'd finally told someone and apprehensive. She didn't want anyone else to learn the truth and then hurt Hailey. "No one knew the truth—just my mom and me.

Hailey learned the truth just a few weeks before she came to me and she's still struggling. She's the one who doesn't want people to know and I'm trying to honor her wishes—but I'm starting to think maybe it's not a good idea to keep it hidden." Her thoughts strayed to Wade and how disappointed he'd be in her when he learned that she'd kept the truth from him.

"I'm sorry you're going through this right now," Liv said as she put her hand on Valerie's arm. "No one knew about Miley, either. Just my immediate family. I couldn't tell anyone the truth. I came to Timber Falls after I gave birth to her and finished my senior year here. No one had any idea I had given up a baby. After college, I came back to take care of my aunt and started a design firm and a wedding-and-events business with Piper. I hadn't even told her—my best friend—that I had a baby. It ate me alive, Valerie. So, please know that I understand, and your secret is safe with me. When it's the right time, you and Hailey will know, and people will understand."

"I hope you're right. I don't want to hurt anyone else. I've already hurt Hailey more than I ever intended."

"She'll understand—maybe not today—but someday. She'll be an adult and she'll realize that life isn't as easy as it seems when you're a kid." She smiled. "Thank you for trusting me with the truth. I'm here for you if you want to talk."

Wade entered the church with his kids and their gazes locked on each other almost immediately. Warmth and happiness filled her chest—but she tried to push the feelings aside. She couldn't act on them—for her sake and for Hailey's.

"Thank you," Valerie said to Liv. "I'm sorry if I burdened you."

"Please don't worry," she said. "I really do understand."

Wade moved toward them, and he smiled. "I hope I'm not interrupting something important."

Valerie shook her head. "Of course not."

"I'm going to take Natalie to childcare," Liv said to Valerie after saying hello to Wade. "I'll talk to you later."

"Bye."

"Thanks again for taking care of the kids yesterday while I worked at your place," Wade said to Valerie after Liv had left.

"My pleasure. We're looking forward to having you over for lunch after church so you can finish up the project."

"Issy and Brayden have not stopped talking about how much fun they had yesterday, and how much more fun they'll have this afternoon." His smile was bright. "We might have to look for excuses to get them together after I'm done on the tree house."

"I don't think it'll be hard." She returned his smile. "Since the girls see each other every day in school."

He nodded as the three kids found them near the coffee bar.

"We're going to sit down," Issy said to her dad with a little giggle as she looked from him to Valerie. "We'll save you two spots right next to each other."

The girls ran off, their giggles following them.

Wade turned to Valerie with an apologetic shrug, and she suddenly understood the giggles.

Issy was playing matchmaker—and by the look on Hailey's face, Valerie suspected that Hailey was in on it, too.

That wasn't good. She couldn't let her daughter down again, and as soon as Hailey learned that Valerie had no interest in dating—or getting married—she'd be upset.

Valerie would have to let her daughter know it wasn't going to happen—and perhaps she had to tell Wade, too.

Though that prospect left her feeling more nervous than ever.

Wade stood in the large tree house and made a final inspection. The sun was starting to dip toward the horizon, and it would soon be dark. He had spent the past four-and-a-half hours finishing up the interior repairs to the tree house and wanted to make sure everything was done before he called Valerie and the kids up to inspect it.

Whoever had originally built the tree house had done an incredible job. It was about eight feet by eight feet and was tall enough for him to stand up comfortably. There were two windows opposite each other, one looking at the backyard and the other looking toward the alley behind the house, with the rooftops of neighboring homes crowding the view. A small deck at the front could hold two grown people and a ladder had been cleverly built up the trunk of the tree to the deck. Wade had fixed a couple of the ladder rungs and a few of the floorboards, but the rest of the structure was solid. It wasn't warm, but the walls, windows and roof kept the worst of the wind out and it was somewhat pleasant. In the summer, it would even be nice.

He climbed down the ladder and put his

tools inside his toolbox before heading toward the back door.

Valerie was in the kitchen, which is where he had found her almost every time he came into the house. She seemed happiest there, cooking or baking. The rest of the house was quiet, which meant the kids were probably upstairs. Valerie was leaning against the counter with a cookbook in hand—but when she looked up at Wade, her smile stopped him in his tracks.

Her cheeks were pink and her blue eyes sparkled. He liked to think they shone for him—but he knew better than to make assumptions. She appeared to like him—but she had given him no indication that her feelings ran deeper. And it was better that way.

"I'm finished," he said. "Want to check it out before we let the kids know?"

"Sure." She set her cookbook on the counter. "They're watching a movie in my bedroom—I hope that's okay."

"That's okay by me. They've been busy

this weekend. I'm sure they are enjoying a little quiet time."

She nodded. "I'll grab my coat."

A couple minutes later, she was climbing up the ladder in front of him and they were soon standing on the deck of the tree house.

"Wow," she said as she looked at her yard and house. "I hadn't realized how high this was. It's a good thing I'm not afraid of heights."

"And I was even farther up on the roof."

"Are *you* afraid of heights?"

"It's hard to be when you're in construction for a living." He opened the door into the tree house. "Ladies first."

She preceded him inside and her eyes grew wide. "This looks amazing! I had no idea how nice this was inside here."

"I replaced a few boards but, for the most part, it's pretty solid. I think Hailey will love it."

"I'm sure she will—I might even confiscate this tree house for myself. It's so peaceful up here." She stood at the window and looked out at her yard. "I could get used to this."

"I'm glad that you're happy," he said, enjoying watching her reaction to the tree house.

She turned and her pleasure was evident in the slope of her smile. "Thank you for all your hard work."

"My pleasure. Hopefully, we can get the kindergarten classroom done soon and then I can get out of your way."

Something flickered in her gaze—something like disappointment. Didn't she want him out of her way?

He was suddenly aware of how alone they were—and the tree house, which had felt large before, seemed a lot smaller.

"It's been so nice getting to know you," she said. "You haven't been in my way at all."

"I'm happy to hear that." He hadn't brought up Thanksgiving dinner again—but maybe now was a good time. "Have you had time to think about Thanksgiving?"

She lowered her gaze—and disappointment sliced through Wade stronger than he expected. Had he really gotten his hopes up that high?

But when she lifted her beautiful blue eyes, he saw something else there—excitement, yet uncertainty. "I appreciate your invitation." She lifted her chin and he saw that look she'd given him when they first met, and she was the principal. Discipline. "Hailey and I would be happy to accept, but I need you to know—I'm almost embarrassed to say it—but it's important."

"What?" He frowned. What could be so serious?

Her cheeks colored and she looked down at her hands for a moment. "I don't want you to think that my acceptance is an indication that I'm interested in you romantically."

His mouth slipped open in surprise as he stared at her. "I didn't—I wouldn't."

"I didn't think so, but I couldn't take the risk." She spoke quickly—embarrassment coloring her words. "I just needed to be up-front, so there wasn't any misunderstanding."

His own embarrassment filled his chest with heat, and he shook his head. "No misunderstanding here."

"Good." She nodded. "I like you, Wade— very much—but I can't date my student's father. And with Hailey recently coming to live with me, I don't have space in my life for—"

"You don't need to say anything more, Valerie." He lifted his hand to stop her from embarrassing both of them further. "I am in the same place."

She smiled—but it was an awkward, stiff smile. "As long as we're both on the same page. I just find it's better to be up-front at the beginning, even if it's uncomfortable, so there are no hurt feelings or misunderstandings."

His embarrassment faded and amusement soon followed. "It's refreshing to meet someone who is honest and up-front. It's not something that most people are good at."

She lowered her gaze again—as if she was uncomfortable being called honest and up-front.

"I hope I didn't offend you," he said quickly.

"No. Of course not. I appreciate honesty, too." She paused, as if she wanted to say more, but then smiled instead.

"I'm happy that we could have this conversation," he said. "I really do appreciate that you felt comfortable enough with me to be straightforward."

"I think the girls will be good friends for a long time," she said. "I think it's important that we can be frank with one another and figure things out as we go."

"I agree." He leaned against the windowsill and said, "So, you're coming to Thanksgiving dinner?"

"If you'll have us," she said.

"Of course. I'm looking forward to it."

"Can I bring anything?"

"Whatever you'd like to contribute."

"How about some pies?"

"That would be great. I'll take care of the rest—but I can't promise it'll be anything compared to your cooking."

Her smile returned and she said, "I'm sure it will be wonderful."

Knowing that Valerie and Hailey would join them made it the best Thanksgiving he'd had in a long time—and it hadn't even happened yet.

He appreciated her honesty—even if he was a little sad that she wasn't interested in more.

But it was best this way—at least, that's what he had to keep telling himself.

"Should we get the kids?" she asked. "And show them the tree house?"

"Absolutely."

They climbed down the ladder again and went into the house to get the kids.

A few minutes later, with coats and

boots on, the kids ran out of the house and climbed the ladder ahead of Wade and Valerie.

Even before they entered, the kids were exclaiming with excitement.

"Wow!" Hailey said. "This is all mine?"

"It's all yours," Valerie said as she turned to Wade, a look of concern in her gaze. "Can this tree house hold all of us?"

"I don't see why not," he said.

"Can I sleep up here?" Hailey asked Valerie.

"Um." She squinted. "I don't think so— at least, not until you're a lot older."

"How old?"

"Thirteen?"

Hailey threw back her head and groaned. "That's forever away."

"We can play up here all the time," Issy said to Hailey. "We can play with our dolls and make believe it's our own house."

The girls began to dream and scheme about all the things they'd do in the tree house and Wade could only smile to himself. He was thankful Hailey had come into Issy's life—and that Valerie had come with her.

Even if they were only going to be friends, it was enough.

At least for now.

Chapter Eight

The house was full of the scent of spices as Valerie stood in her kitchen on Thanksgiving Day. She'd let Hailey sleep in again, but the little girl was now in the kitchen with her, rolling out pastry dough on the counter. A smudge of flour was on her nose and she wore one of Valerie's large aprons.

"I love baking," Hailey said to Valerie. "Mom never baked."

"I know." Valerie smiled as she pared an apple into small pieces. "I had to teach myself when I was about your age. Mom didn't do a lot of cooking. When I was ten, I was making most of our meals."

Hailey glanced up at Valerie and gave her an odd look.

"What?" Valerie asked as she stopped paring the apple.

"It's weird that she is your mom, too."

"She was young when she had me. Eighteen—just like I was when you were born. She was only thirty-six when you came along. For a long time, it was just the two of us—kind of like how it was just the two of you and now it's just the two of us."

Hailey continued to roll the dough, but she seemed deep in thought. "Did you ever want a dad? Or brothers and sisters?"

"All the time."

"Me too." She shrugged. "Lyle was kind of like a dad for a little while, but he was so old, he didn't like to do anything fun. He wanted to play board games and cards all the time. I want a dad like—" She paused.

"Like?" Valerie asked.

"Like Issy's dad. Lyle would never get on the roof of a tree house or go sledding or play baseball. Issy said her dad likes to do a lot of fun things. In the summer, they even go swimming behind their house."

Valerie finished paring the apple and began to measure out the sugar into the bowl. "Mr. Griffin seems like a really good dad." She had been looking for an opportunity to tell Hailey that she need not get her hopes up about Wade—but she needed to be careful and wise, so Hailey wouldn't get upset.

"I've never spent Thanksgiving with a family before," Hailey said.

Pain sliced through Valerie's heart as she placed her hand on Hailey's cheek. "I wish I could have given you a family—but both of us need to be happy with the family we have. This one. You and me. I know you and Issy are hopeful that Mr. Griffin and I will start to date—or even get married— but I have no interest in doing either. I'm sorry."

Hailey looked up at Valerie and blinked a couple of times before she moved away from Valerie's touch.

"Can I call Mom?" Hailey asked.

The little girl hadn't asked to talk to her mom before now—and her mom hadn't made an effort to call. But it was Thanksgiving—a perfect time to reach out.

"Of course."

Hailey jumped up and down with excitement as Valerie took her cell phone off the counter and found her mom's phone number. She put it on speakerphone as they waited for an answer.

"Hello," her mom said a couple seconds later.

"Hi, Mom," Valerie said.

"Hi, Mom!" Hailey chimed in.

"This is a nice surprise," her mom said. "How are you two doing?"

"Great." Valerie leaned against the counter. "We're making pies."

"To take to my friend's house," Hailey added. "She has a dad and a little brother."

"That sounds nice."

"What are you doing today?" Hailey asked.

"Lyle and I are going to a Thanksgiving meal at the community center in our retirement complex. It's so beautiful here. Nice and warm with lots of sun." Her mom told them all about the home they were living in and the activities that kept them busy, from pickleball to water aerobics, karaoke night and bingo.

The more she spoke, the sadder Hailey's face became.

"Things are going well here," Valerie said, needing to remind Hailey that her life was full, too. "Hailey is making a lot of great friends and doing well in school."

"I'm so happy to hear that. It's good to hear from both of you. I've been quiet on my end, trying to give you two time to get to know one another."

"I miss you," Hailey said as she began to cry. "Can I come live with you in Arizona?"

Valerie's heart twisted as she put her hand on Hailey's shoulder.

"I'm sorry, sweetheart," her mom said.

"Living with your real mom is the best thing for you. We shouldn't have let it go on as long as we did. But it sounds like you're doing well there, and you're making friends. That's what I hoped."

Hailey continued to cry as she begged her mom to let her move in with her and Lyle.

"Hailey," her mom said in a firm voice, "this is why I didn't call before now. It's best for you to stay in Timber Falls with Valerie. I know it's hard, but one day, you'll thank me. I promise. Keep your chin up and look for all the good in your life."

"Can I call you again?" Hailey asked.

"If your mom says it's okay." She paused and then said, "Valerie?"

"Yes?" Valerie asked.

"Can you take me off speakerphone so I can talk to you in private?"

"Of course."

"Goodbye, Hailey," her mom said. "I love you."

"I love you, too." Hailey wiped at her

tears as she watched Valerie take the phone off speakerphone.

"Okay," Valerie said to her mom. "You're off speaker."

"Good." Her mom sighed. "I'm sorry Hailey is struggling. I imagine you are, too. But I raised two very strong and brave girls. I know you two can do this."

"It hasn't been easy, but we're figuring things out."

"I had a feeling you were. Now, I don't mind if Hailey calls me—but I don't think it's a good idea if she calls all the time. She needs to learn how to go to you with her problems, as well as her highs and lows. I miss her very much, but I'm trying to give you both space."

"I know."

"I want you to use your best judgment when she calls. If it's just to say hi and catch up, that's one thing. If she's relying too heavily on me, that's another thing."

"I agree."

"Good. It was nice hearing from both of

you today. I hope you have a nice Thanksgiving."

"You too. Bye, Mom."

"Bye, Valerie. Love you."

"Love you too."

Valerie hung up the phone and met Hailey's sad gaze.

"Can I hug you?" Valerie asked her daughter. "I need a hug."

It took Hailey a moment, but she finally nodded.

Valerie opened her arms and Hailey walked into her embrace.

Warmth filled Valerie as Hailey's arms folded around her and held her tight.

They stood that way for several seconds, and then Hailey pulled away.

"Can we make another pie?" she asked. "A pumpkin one now?"

"Let's finish up the apple one," Valerie said, "and then we'll make a pumpkin and a peanut butter one, too."

"That's a lot of pie."

"It's the best part of Thanksgiving—and it makes good leftovers, too."

Hailey smiled and wiped at her tears again. "I like baking with you."

"I like baking with you, too."

They put the apple pie together and Valerie showed Hailey how to create a latticework of pastry across the top before putting it into the oven.

"We'll bake it for about thirty-five minutes and then we'll let it cool to take to the Griffins'."

As Valerie pulled together all the ingredients they'd need for the pumpkin pie, Hailey cleaned up the mess they'd made with the apple pie. They worked in quiet companionship as the scent of apple, cinnamon and nutmeg filled the air.

When everything was ready to start the pumpkin pie, Hailey glanced up at Valerie again, looking a little shy.

"Can I tell you something?"

"You can tell me anything, Hailey."

"Issy *does* want you to marry her dad.

And so do I. She told me she wants you to marry her dad so that you can be her mom and I can be her sister. But you don't want to marry her dad?"

"No—I mean, I don't know." She shook her head, feeling flustered and embarrassed, even though they'd already discussed this. She should have known Hailey wouldn't let it go so easily. "I mean, no. I have no intentions of marrying anyone."

"But if you *did* want to get married, would you want to marry Mr. Griffin?"

"Hailey," Valerie warned, yet, as she thought about the question, she couldn't help but wonder. If she *was* in a position to get married—would Wade be the kind of man she might fall in love with? He was easy to talk to, kind, thoughtful, hardworking. He was well-respected in the community and never failed to follow through with his commitments. He did an admirable job raising his children as a single dad and he was handsome, as well. *If* she had ever wanted to get married, Wade would be the kind of man she'd look for.

"Why don't you want to marry him?" Hailey asked, frowning.

"It's complicated, Hailey. And, besides, I don't know how he feels about me." She thought back to their conversation in the tree house. She had been blunt when she told him they had to keep things on a friendly level—but it had been necessary. He had seemed surprised—but had he been disappointed? It was hard to tell. Had she wanted him to be disappointed?

"I think he likes you. Issy says he likes you. And he invited us to have Thanksgiving with them. Issy said no woman has ever had Thanksgiving with them."

"I think he felt obligated to invite us."

"What does that mean?"

"He wasn't given a choice. But it doesn't matter. You don't need to worry about me getting married."

"I'm not worried. I want you to get married. And I want Issy to live with us."

Valerie needed to get the conversation back to safe waters, so she steered it in a different direction. "We need to focus on getting used to each other before we talk about bringing anyone else into our family. Okay?"

Hailey's shoulders fell. "Okay."

"I love having you in my life, Hailey. At first, it felt scary, but now it feels like we're right where we belong. Together."

She nodded, but looked down at the ingredients on the counter. "I'm still sad—but I like that you make breakfast for me every morning and that the house is always clean and that you teach me how to bake things."

It was the first good thing Hailey had said about living with her, and she wasn't going to take it for granted. "I love all those things, too. I love having someone to make breakfast for, and someone to clean up after, and someone to bake with. Although, I wouldn't mind if you did a little more cleaning up after yourself."

Hailey's smile was bright as she began to giggle.

"And I love Annabelle," Hailey said, which caused the dog to perk up from her bed in the corner of the kitchen, near the warm heater vent. "And the tree house, and my teacher and my favorite friend, Issy."

"It sounds like you've found some wonderful things to be thankful for."

"Mom said I should look for the good things," Hailey said. "So I am."

"Mom was right." Valerie was happy they had called her mom—even if it had been hard. "And now," Valerie added, "we have something else to look forward to."

"Going to Issy's house!" Hailey said.

"Exactly." Valerie wasn't sure how things would go at the Griffins' house—but she had a feeling they were going to have a great time.

Wade looked at the clock on the microwave for the fifth time in the past thirty minutes. The house smelled like roasting turkey, sage dressing and baked yams. He'd been up since five that morning, making sure that everything was on track to be ready by suppertime. They'd left for a little while to have brunch at his parents' house, and then they had come back home.

As the turkey roasted, Wade had put his kids to work helping him clean the house. They had vacuumed, dusted, picked up toys, wiped down walls and swept. It was easy to get them to help when they were excited that they'd have guests. Wade couldn't remember the last time they'd had people over who weren't family.

They were also helpful in the kitchen, when able, and they had happily set the table for the five of them.

"Should I set a place for Annabelle?" Brayden asked Wade as he put a plate on the table.

"No." Wade shook his head. "I don't even know if she's bringing Annabelle—

but if she does, Annabelle will stay on the ground."

"She might not bring Annabelle?" Brayden asked, his eyes growing wide. "But we invited Annabelle to come!"

Wade saw a meltdown coming, and since he didn't mind if the dog joined Valerie and Hailey, he picked up his phone to send Valerie a quick text.

Brayden wants me to remind you that Annabelle is invited to come to supper.

"There," Wade said, "I sent Miss Wilmington a reminder that Annabelle is invited."

Brayden's frown disappeared and he grinned.

Wade hadn't felt this nervous in years.

"Hello!" a woman said as she entered the foyer. "Wade?"

"Mom?" Wade frowned as he left the kitchen and entered the foyer. "What are you doing here?"

His dad walked through the door next and closed it behind him.

"Bingo was canceled," his mom said with a frown. "Apparently, there was a small fire in the American Legion's kitchen."

"Tom already called me," his dad said as he took his coat off and hung it on the coat-tree, referencing the Legion's manager. "I'll send a crew there tomorrow morning and look at the damage. We'll have another job."

"Grammy!" Brayden said as he came into the foyer. He threw himself into her arms, even though he had just been at her house a couple hours ago.

"Hey, buddy," his mom said. "Happy Thanksgiving again."

"Happy Thanksgiving!" Brayden said. "We have a dog coming for supper."

"A dog?" His mom frowned and looked from Brayden to Wade. "What kind of dog?"

"A little white one," Brayden said.

"You have company coming?" his dad asked.

"Yes—I do." He hadn't told his parents about Valerie and Hailey's plans to come. He wasn't sure why, although he was certain his mom would make too big a deal about it.

"Oh?" His mom stood straight, tilting her head in curiosity. "Someone I know?"

"It's Miss Wilmington!" Brayden said. "And her dog, Annabelle."

"Valerie Wilmington?" His mom's eyebrows rose high. "Why didn't you say something?"

"It's not a big deal." Wade shrugged, trying to sound nonchalant. "Her sister, Hailey, has become good friends with Issy and Issy asked if they could come over."

"Not a big deal?" His mom took off her coat and handed it to his dad. "This is a huge deal."

"What are you doing?" Wade asked.

"We're staying for Thanksgiving supper." His mom left the foyer and walked into the kitchen. "And now that I know who is coming, I'm actually happy bingo was canceled."

"Ruth," Wade's dad said, "do you want me to bring in the pies you brought?"

"Valerie is bringing pies," Wade said.

"You better bring them in," his mom told his dad. "Who knows how her pies will taste. I don't want Thanksgiving ruined because the pies are bad."

"Mom," Wade said with a warning in his voice. "Valerie is an excellent cook. We don't need your pies."

His mom gave him a look, but then lifted her hands and said, "Fine. We'll take our chances."

"Grammy!" Issy said as she ran down the hallway from her bedroom. "You're here."

"Surprise." His mom gave Issy a hug and turned to Wade. "Now—let's see what needs to be done. When is Valerie coming?"

"Any minute. Supper's almost ready."

"I got here just in time then." His mom went to the stove and lifted the lids to look at each dish. "Your potatoes could use a little more butter and your stuffing needs some chicken stock. It looks too dry. How is the turkey?"

"It's fine, Mom." Wade was feeling nervous before—but now, he was panicked. His parents rarely used a filter when they spoke to people. They said what they wanted, when they wanted and how they wanted. What if they said something inappropriate to Valerie or Hailey? He couldn't ask his parents to leave—but he wished they had called before coming.

"Just give me a few minutes and I'll get everything whipped into shape." She frowned. "Where is your gravy?"

"Gravy?" Wade palmed his forehead. "I forgot the gravy."

"It looks like I *did* get here just in time." She rolled up her sleeves and then took over Wade's kitchen, chatting nonstop as she worked.

His dad took a seat in the living room, which was connected to the kitchen, and turned on the TV to the Vikings game.

"Dad," Wade said. "I was hoping to keep the television off today."

"Don't worry about me," his dad said. "I don't need to be gossiping in the kitchen with your mom."

"Oh, Fred," his mom said as she rolled her eyes. "I'm not a gossiper."

"At least turn down the volume," Wade protested.

His dad grumbled and then turned down the volume.

The doorbell rang and Wade's pulse escalated. "It's Valerie."

"They're here!" Issy said as she ran through the kitchen and into the foyer.

"Annabelle!" Brayden rushed into the foyer to see if the Wilmingtons had brought their dog. "Annabelle, Annabelle, Annabelle!"

"Please," Wade said to his parents, wishing his house didn't feel so chaotic. "Don't embarrass me."

His mom rolled her eyes, as if that was a preposterous statement, and his dad ignored him.

Wade took a deep breath and then left the kitchen to enter the foyer.

Brayden was already on the ground with Annabelle, who was wagging her tail. Valerie was holding a double-pie carrier and Hailey had a single one in her hands. Valerie's smile was brilliant as she said, "Happy Thanksgiving." She looked beautiful in a long wool coat, her blond hair slightly curled and she wore pearl earrings.

"Happy Thanksgiving," Wade said. "Can I take that?"

She handed him the double-pie carrier. "We went a little overboard and made three pies. I hope that's okay."

"It's great." He took the single pie from Hailey, who immediately took off her coat with Issy's help. "You could have brought six and I would have been happy."

Valerie also began to remove her coat. She was wearing a green dress with an oversize scarf around her neck and shoulders. Wade wished his parents hadn't come—because then he could enjoy Valerie's attention. Now, he'd have to share it with his mom, who loved nothing more than to talk. "My parents' plans changed, and they were able to join us. I hope you don't mind."

"Mind?" Valerie smiled. "Of course not."

He couldn't tell if she was disappointed or uncomfortable—or if she really didn't mind. Her smile never faltered.

Wade would have been happy to just stand in the foyer and not bring his parents into the conversation—but that would be impossible.

"Come on in," Wade said.

Valerie hung up her coat and then took the single pie back from Wade.

Their hands brushed and he met her

gaze. She glanced at him, her cheeks turning pink, and smiled.

"I'm so happy you're here," Issy said to Hailey. "I can't wait to show you my room."

The two little girls ran off together and Brayden took Annabelle into his arms and disappeared into the kitchen.

For a split second, it was just Wade and Valerie in the foyer and Wade said, "I'm sorry if my parents make you feel uncomfortable. My mom's really excited you're here—I think she might think there's something going on between us. I tried telling her there's nothing—but she can be pretty stubborn when she wants to be. And my dad is—just my dad."

Valerie nodded and chuckled. "Enough said. I understand."

His relief was momentary—because as soon as they entered the kitchen, he saw the look his mom gave Valerie.

She had that matchmaking gleam in her eyes—the one he'd seen many times as she tried to pair unsuspecting singles in their church.

"Hello, Valerie!" his mom said as she pulled Valerie into a hug without asking.

Valerie had to balance the pie in her hand as she accepted the hug like a long-lost daughter. "Hello, Mrs. Griffin."

"Oh, call me Ruth." She pulled back but put her hands on Valerie's upper arms. "Once we share a holiday together, we're practically family."

Wade tried not to groan.

"Hello," his dad called from the couch.

"Hello," Valerie replied.

"I hope Wade didn't force you here against your will."

"Dad." Wade shook his head. "That's not even funny."

Valerie bit her bottom lip, as if she was trying not to smile.

"What?" his dad asked. "She's the first woman you've brought into your house since your wife left. I thought you might be getting desperate."

"Oh, Fred." His mom waved his comment aside and then said to Valerie, "Don't listen to him. Besides, you're not the kind of girl Wade would invite over if he was desperate." She took the pie out of Valerie's hand. "Wade told me you were bringing the pies. Let's just have a peek, shall we?"

Valerie's eyes were wide at his parents' comments—and when she looked at Wade, he shrugged and mouthed, "I'm sorry."

His mom set the pie on the counter and lifted the lid. Her eyes started to shine. "What a pretty pie. Where did you buy it?"

"I made it," Valerie said. "With Hailey's help. We made all three pies."

"My oh my." His mom lifted an eyebrow and said in a mock-tease, "Aren't we an overachiever. Perhaps trying to impress Wade?"

"It looks delicious," Wade said quickly. "I think supper is about ready. I hope you're hungry."

"I'm starving," Valerie said, just as quickly. "What can I do to help?"

"Nothing, dear," his mom said. "I have it all under control. I just need to finish up the gravy and then we'll be ready to go."

"At least let me help carry the food to the table," Valerie protested.

"That's a perfect idea." His mom grabbed the bread basket and handed it to Valerie. "I'll look after the rest of the meal, and you and Wade can take it to the dining room."

Wade grabbed the cranberries and the yams and said to Valerie, "I'll show you where to take cover—I mean, where the dining room is."

She giggled and he was relieved to see she was finding his parents funny—and not insulting. But the night was young.

His house had been added on to many times over the years, so the dining room faced the river, on the other side of the living room. It offered Wade a few seconds to apologize to Valerie.

"I'm sorry for my parents," he said. "There's really no excuse for them."

Valerie laid her hand on Wade's arm—and he stilled instantly.

"It's okay," she said. "I've had my fair share of difficult parents in my career. I know how to handle them."

The touch of her hand felt like fire against his skin, and he had to focus hard to concentrate on her words. "Thanks for understanding."

She smiled and looked down at her hand before removing it.

As she walked back to the kitchen, she clasped her hands together—and he wondered if she had felt what he had felt.

Despite the fact that his parents were there, he was looking forward to the rest of the evening.

He just hoped his mom and dad wouldn't embarrass him even more.

Chapter Nine

"The meal was delicious," Valerie said to Ruth, her stomach full of good food as they sat at the dining-room table. "I'd love your dressing recipe."

"I didn't make it," Ruth said as she nodded at Wade, who sat at the head of the table. "Wade made everything, except the gravy." She leaned closer to Valerie and said in a mock-whisper, "I added a little chicken stock to fluff up the dressing a bit—but the rest is all Wade."

Valerie turned to Wade. "You made most of the meal?"

He nodded, sitting back in his chair, his

plate empty. "I had some help, of course." He smiled at his kids, who were waiting for pie. "Brayden helped make the bread-crumbs and Issy helped chop the celery."

"Well done," Valerie said to the kids. "I loved it."

Their faces beamed with pride.

"Has anyone saved room for pie?" Valerie asked. "Or should we wait a bit for dessert?"

"I always have room for pie," Fred said from his place at the table. He patted his stomach, which was a little thick, but he seemed to stay active with his construction company. "Especially pumpkin with a dab of whipped cream."

"I'll grab the pies," Valerie said as she started to rise.

"Let me help." Wade also stood and they cleared a few of the empty dishes from the table before heading into the kitchen.

"We'll keep the kids occupied," Ruth called to them. "Take your time."

"Getting pies?" Wade asked.

Ruth winked at him—and Valerie's cheeks grew warm. What must they be thinking? Their teasing and innuendos had started the moment they arrived and were ongoing. Would everyone else think Wade and Valerie were dating when Ruth told the church ladies she had come for Thanksgiving? Because Valerie was certain Ruth would tell them—if she hadn't already texted them with the news.

Valerie glanced at Wade as they set the dirty dishes on the counter near the sink. His smile was so sweet. For a second, she didn't mind if people thought they were dating. She would be honored to be mentioned in the same sentence as Wade Griffin.

Yet—the same niggling doubt wound its way around her heart. There was so much he didn't know about her—so much she didn't know about him. And, besides that, she wasn't in a place to let this grow.

Wade went to the refrigerator to get out the peanut-butter pie while Valerie took the lid off the pie carrier and removed the apple and pumpkin pies onto the counter to cut.

A buzzing noise came from her purse, which was sitting on a nearby counter.

"Who would be calling me on Thanksgiving?" Valerie asked with a frown, more to herself than Wade. Was it her mom? She doubted it, since they'd already spoken that day.

Wade glanced at her briefly before he set the peanut-butter pie on the counter next to the others.

Valerie pulled her phone out of her purse and frowned. She didn't recognize the number, but it had a local area code. It might be a spam call—but she wasn't taking any risks. If someone local was calling her today, it was probably important.

"Hello," she said tentatively.

"Miss Wilmington?" a female voice asked on the other end.

"Yes. Who is this?"

"It's Sandra Cole."

"Oh. Hello, Mrs. Cole." Sandra was the music teacher at Timber Falls Christian School. She was an older woman, close to retirement age, who had stepped in to teach when the school opened three years ago. Valerie hadn't gotten to know her as well as some of the other teachers, but everyone glowed with appreciation when they talked about her. The kids especially loved Mrs. Cole. "Happy Thanksgiving. I hope everything is okay."

"I wish it was." Her voice was heavy with grief.

Valerie frowned and noticed that Wade was watching her with concern.

"What's wrong?" Valerie asked Mrs. Cole.

"My daughter in Oklahoma was expecting a baby, her fourth child. She went into premature labor early this morning. The baby wasn't due until the end of February, but they weren't able to stop her labor. She gave birth to a little girl who is just over two pounds. She's fighting for her life and my daughter needs me. My husband and I are driving to the airport as we speak."

"Oh, my," Valerie said, leaning against the counter. "I'm so sorry to hear that. I will be praying for all of you."

"Thank you," Mrs. Cole said. "I know it's Thanksgiving, but I wanted to tell you as soon as possible, since you'll need to find a long-term substitute teacher for me. I will be in Oklahoma as long as my daughter needs me, and with three little ones under the age of five, she'll probably need me for several months."

"Several months?" Valerie wished she was next to one of the island stools. She needed to sit down.

"And now, right before the Christmas season—I'm so sorry, Miss Wilmington. I know this puts you in a tough position. But, please know that I will be available by phone, if you need anything. I'm sure you know how bad I feel—but I must go to my daughter. She's my priority right now."

"I completely understand. Please don't

waste any energy worrying or fretting about school. I'll do everything on my end to make sure your class is taken care of. You just focus on your daughter and grandchildren."

"Thank you so much." Mrs. Cole's voice was shaky with tears. "You don't know how much I appreciate your help."

"Of course. One of the mottos of our school is that family comes first. For the students—*and* the teachers. Thank you for calling and giving me time to work on this. Please let me know if there's anything else we can do for you and your family right now."

"I will. Thank you, again. I hope you have a happy Thanksgiving."

"You too—as much as you can. Keep me informed."

"Goodbye, Miss Wilmington."

"Goodbye." Valerie hung up the phone and looked at it for a moment, trying to pull her thoughts together.

"It sounds like Mrs. Cole is dealing with a family crisis?" Wade asked gently.

"Her daughter gave birth to a baby several months early and she's on her way to Oklahoma to help."

"I'm sorry to hear that."

"So am I." Valerie put her phone back in her purse. "Not only for her family's sake, but because I now have to find a long-term music teacher sub. And right before Christmas. One of the busiest school months."

Ruth entered the kitchen, her eyes wide with concern. "Did I hear that Sandra Cole's daughter gave birth too early? Oh, that's too bad. We've been praying for her. Sandra put her on the church prayer list last week when there were some complications."

"I'm afraid so," Valerie said. "And now I need to find a long-term music substitute."

"I know who you could ask," Ruth said.

Valerie felt a rush of relief at the assurance in Ruth's voice. "Who?"

"Wade."

Both ladies turned to look at Wade.

He frowned. *"Me?"*

"You have a degree in music composition," Ruth said. "You could put it to use and help the school."

"But I have a job, Mom."

"A job that gets very slow over the winter," she countered. "This would be perfect for you, Wade. You could put your expensive degree to use, help the school and make a little extra money during the tight months."

"What's this?" Fred asked as he entered the kitchen, frowning. "What are you trying to talk Wade into doing?"

"Nothing," Wade said, shaking his head.

"We're trying to talk him into being a substitute music teacher for the school," Ruth told her husband.

Valerie watched Wade carefully to gauge whether he would be interested. In Minnesota, a niche position that was hard to fill, like theater, music, dance, or visual arts could be filled by a person without a teaching degree, if the school hiring the substitute petitioned the state on their behalf. They could obtain a one-year license, which often helped the school until a permanent teacher could be hired. With Wade's background in music, and his connection to the school and church, he would be a great candidate for a long-term sub.

But, only if he wanted the job. And by the look on his face—and his father's face—she wasn't sure he did.

"A substitute *music* teacher?" Fred asked, wrinkling his nose, as if it was the worst idea he'd ever heard. "Who wants to teach music to little kids all day?"

"At one point, Wade," Ruth said.

"You wanted to be a teacher?" Fred asked his son.

"I wanted to do something with music," Wade acknowledged. "I threw around the idea of teaching for a while, but nothing ever panned out."

"Because you wised up and came to

work for me," Fred said. "Doing something worthwhile and useful with your time."

"Teaching music is worthwhile and useful," Wade told his dad, the color rising in his cheeks. "It's just as honorable as any other profession."

"It's a—"

Ruth laid her hand on Fred's arm and shook her head. "Remember that this is Wade's house, and Miss Wilmington is the principal of the school where our grandchildren—who are in the next room— attend. With one comment, you could possibly insult every person in this house."

Fred pressed his mouth together, but Valerie could tell it took a lot of effort.

"None of this matters," Wade said as his calm voice seemed to settle the matter. "Valerie didn't ask me to be the substitute teacher—and, even if she did, I'm not sure it would be a good idea."

Everyone looked at Valerie and she simply smiled. She wanted to ask Wade to be the substitute—but she wasn't going to have this conversation in front of his parents.

"Who is ready for pie?" she asked instead.

Wade gave her an appreciative smile and she returned it.

As soon as his parents were gone, she would ask him to take the position. She tried telling herself it was only because he would do an exceptional job—which was true—but she knew the truth. His construction project at the school would be done on Monday morning and she liked the idea of having a reason to keep seeing him.

After the supper dishes were washed and put away, the kids begged to play some games. Wade's parents stayed long enough for his mom to play several rounds of Candyland and slapjack, while his dad snoozed on the couch watching more football.

Wade sat at the dining-room table with

the kids, his mom, and Valerie, and enjoyed playing board games. But he couldn't shake what had happened earlier. There was a part of him that wanted to step in and substitute for Mrs. Cole. It was a great opportunity to use his education—and see if it was something he might want to do full-time. Ever since Issy had been born, he hadn't taken the risk of using his music degree. There hadn't been an opportunity and he needed to be smart.

But this was different. There was so little work in construction during the winter that it was the perfect time to try something new.

If his dad didn't put up a fuss. Wade was nervous to admit to his father that he was considering the job—*if* Valerie offered it to him. A part of him worried his dad would tell him it was the family business or nothing. His mom would back him up—but that wasn't always enough where his father was concerned.

No matter what, he would have to think

hard about the opportunity. As soon as his parents left, he would bring up the subject with Valerie again. But that meant he needed to make sure she stayed long enough.

"Well," his mom said as she pushed back from the table. "I can hear Grandpa Fred snoring in the living room. We should get home so I can put him to bed."

"It's not bedtime!" Issy protested, glancing at the clock, which said eight.

"It's close," Wade told his daughter.

"But it's a holiday." She blinked her big brown eyes at him. "We don't have school tomorrow. Can't we stay up a little later?"

"Maybe a little bit," Wade said.

Issy and Brayden cheered.

As his mom got up from the table, so did Valerie.

But Wade didn't want her to leave. Not yet.

"Issy," Wade said, "why don't you get out your Apples to Apples Junior game? That would be fun to play next."

"I love Apples to Apples," Hailey said.

"But I can't read the cards!" Brayden said, frowning.

"I'll help you," Valerie offered.

His face brightened. "Okay."

"Bye, kiddos," his mom said.

Issy and Brayden gave her a hug and then Issy went to get the game.

"Goodbye," Valerie said. "It was nice spending the evening with you."

"And you too, dear," his mom said. "I'll see you at church on Sunday."

"I'll be right back," Wade said to Valerie and the kids.

He walked his mom and dad to the front door and gave his mom a hug. "Thanks for your help today."

"My pleasure." She winked at him. "Have fun with the rest of your evening. Valerie is delightful."

"Don't let her talk nonsense into you," his dad said with a frown. "You're a Griffin man. We work with our hands. There isn't a teacher among us."

Wade shook his head at his dad's short-sightedness, but knowing he wouldn't change his opinion with arguing, he simply smiled.

As soon as his parents were gone, Wade sighed in relief.

He entered the kitchen and found Valerie opening the pie carrier again.

Her cheeks reddened, as if she was being caught with her hand in the cookie jar. "It's Thanksgiving," she said with a shrug. "I'm having another piece of pie."

"Sounds good to me." Wade laughed. "I think I'll join you. That peanut-butter pie is outstanding."

"Thank you." She smiled. "The kids are still cleaning up Candyland and setting up Apples to Apples."

Wade pulled out two small plates and some forks. He brought them to the counter and took a seat. He wasn't ready to rejoin the kids—not yet.

Valerie cut two pieces of pie and set them on the plates. Wade had made some decaf coffee after supper, and she helped herself to another half cup before she joined him at the counter.

She sat on the stool next to him. "You have a lovely house, Wade."

"Thank you. I've done a lot of work on it since we moved in."

"I can tell." She cut off a small piece of pie and slipped it into her mouth.

They sat in companionable silence. Wade wanted to know how to bring up the topic of the substitute job, but wasn't sure if she'd even be interested in him taking the position.

"I should apologize for my parents again," he said.

"You don't need to. We don't get to choose our family—at least not all of them."

He thought about her family. He was only aware of her mom—and what he knew about her didn't impress him. Would Valerie mention her?

"I suppose you're right," he said. "But I

still feel responsible for them. I hope they didn't make you feel too uncomfortable."

She smiled at him, revealing her dimples. "I liked how many times you blushed today. Even with your beard, I can see when the color creeps into your cheeks."

He chuckled. "I'm happy my discomfort pleases you."

She laughed. "Sorry."

"I don't think you are," he teased.

Valerie shrugged and took another bite of her pie, her eyes shining.

They were both quiet again, and then Valerie said, "I wanted to stay a bit longer to ask you a question."

Wade's hand stilled as he cut into his pie. What kind of question would make her voice sound so intense?

"Yeah?"

She took a deep breath. "I know this is a big ask—but would you consider taking the substitute job for Mrs. Cole?"

He laid his fork on the plate and turned to her on the stool. "Are you serious?"

"I'm very serious." She also turned to him, her blue eyes studying his. "I've hired dozens of teachers over my career, and I know what it takes to do the job well. You have all the qualities I look for in a teacher. You're hardworking, dependable, kind, smart and creative. I think you'd do an incredible job."

The list of attributes she'd just listed filled Wade with indescribable joy. "You think that highly of me?"

"I think very highly of you, Wade."

His chest felt like it might burst from pleasure. To have a woman like Valerie Wilmington value and esteem him was the greatest gift he could be given. "Thank you. I think very highly of you, too, Valerie."

It was her turn to blush.

"I've never met anyone like you," he continued, risking a lot to reveal the depths of his attraction to her. "You are intelligent, confident, thoughtful, kind and—" He paused, realizing what he was going to say—and then he decided to say it anyway. "And really pretty."

This time, the color was so bright in her cheeks, she looked down at her hands. "Thank you." When she glanced up at him, she said, "Do you think you'd consider taking the job? I'm not sure how long it would last, but even if we could get through the holidays, that would be ideal. The next month is going to be busy. After the new year, we can reassess, try to get a feel from Mrs. Cole as to when she thinks she might return, and then go from there."

"I don't have a teaching degree."

"That's okay." She quickly explained how the process worked. "You can get a special license for one year, which will be more than enough."

"What would the job require? How many hours? What are the expectations?"

"She taught kindergarten through eighth grade. There are two classrooms per grade, and each class has one music lesson a week—so that is sixteen classes spread out over five days. Three classes a day for four days—and four classes on the fifth day. They will begin practicing for the Christmas pageant on Monday. I'm sure Mrs. Cole has all their songs picked out already and will be more than happy to share any other information she has." She smiled. "And I will be on hand to offer any assistance I can. I've seen my fair share of Christmas programs."

Wade thought through all his obligations and responsibilities. This would be a full-time job for the next month. He needed to make sure his dad would be on board, because he couldn't jeopardize his family's business to step up and help the school. Wade knew they could get along without him for a month—especially in December—but his dad was technically his boss and would need to approve the decision.

"I am interested in the position," Wade said. "But I need to take a little bit of time to get things in order and to make sure the construction company can go without my help for the next several weeks."

"I completely understand," Valerie said. "I wouldn't expect you to make a snap decision."

"When do you need to know by?"

"The sooner the better. I could get by with a temporary sub on Monday and Tuesday, but I need someone in place to lead the Christmas program as soon as possible."

"I get it." Wade nodded. "I will try to have an answer for you in the next day or two. Will that be okay?"

"Of course."

"Good."

"Daddy!" Issy said as she joined them in the kitchen. "We're waiting!"

"Coming, Bug." Wade tilted his head toward the dining room and said to Valerie, "How about we see what kind of Apples to Apples skills you have?"

She lifted her eyebrows. "Oh, I have skills."

He grinned. "It's time to prove it."

Valerie took her coffee cup and pie and headed toward the dining room, turning to offer him a smile before she disappeared around the corner.

They spent the next thirty minutes playing Apples to Apples with the kids. Wade loved the laughter around his dining-room table. Issy and Hailey were like two peas in a pod, so alike. They acted as if they'd known each other their whole lives, already sharing inside jokes and little secrets. Brayden held Annabelle as he and Valerie teamed up to play against the other three.

When it was time for Valerie and Hailey to leave, there were complaints all around. Wade was just as disappointed as his kids to see the pair leave, but it was getting late.

"I'll call you when I make a decision," Wade promised Valerie as they walked out the front door.

"I look forward to hearing from you,"

she said as the kids waved goodbye to their visitors.

Wade closed the door, wishing that he had more plans to see Valerie again. He'd see her at church on Sunday, and at the school on Monday—whether he was there as the new music teacher or finishing up the kindergarten classroom, which only needed the countertop to be installed before the class could move back in. But seeing them at church or at school didn't afford him the same kind of quiet, personal time they'd been having at each other's homes.

Yet—the only way to get that was to date her and after talking to her in the tree house, he knew how she felt about that idea.

"Okay, kiddos," Wade said, "time to get ready for bed."

Thirty minutes later, after tucking in his children, he picked up his cell phone to call his dad. Even though his dad had been snoozing on the couch earlier, Wade knew his dad was a night owl and would still be awake watching the late-night news. He never missed it.

Wade pressed his dad's number and paced between the kitchen and living room while he waited for his dad to answer. He said a quiet prayer as he took a deep breath.

"Hey," his dad said as he picked up the call. "What's going on?"

"I'd like to talk to you about the substitute teaching position that opened up at the school."

"You're not seriously considering it, are you?"

"I kind of am. Valerie is in a tight spot with the holidays coming up and the Christmas program just four weeks away. I have the skills to help—and, as one of the parents of children who attend, I think it would be a nice thing to do. December is usually our slowest month with Griffin Construction. I'm hoping you can get along without me for a few weeks."

His dad was quiet on the other end of the phone and Wade's muscles grew tense, waiting.

"Your mom talked to me on the way home," his dad said, though he didn't sound pleased. "She reminded me of all the sacrifices you made when Issy was born and since Amber left. I know music was always important to you and I'm sure you'd enjoy the opportunity to help the school." He paused and Wade held his breath. "I suppose we can get along without you for the next four or five weeks. I might need to call on you for help if we get into a bind—but I'll try my best to hand off the work to someone else."

Wade briefly closed his eyes. "Thanks, Dad. I am excited to see what I can do to help the school." And Valerie—but he wouldn't admit that to his dad.

"I can send Mitchell to the school to finish up the countertop on Monday," his dad continued, mentioning one of their foremen. "If you could stop in and make sure things are getting done to our standard, that would be good."

"Of course. I should be able to do that."

His dad let out a sigh. "I don't know why you want to do this, but I won't stand in your way if you do."

"Thanks, Dad. I appreciate your flexibility."

"Thank your mom. She's the one who practically forced me into this decision."

Wade shook his head at his dad's inability to be soft. "I'll talk to you later."

"Bye."

They got off the phone and Wade stood for a minute in his kitchen, letting the decision sink in. He never dreamed he'd get the chance to pursue his love for music—and never as an elementary-and-middle-school teacher. But God had a funny way of working things out.

He couldn't wait to tell Valerie what he decided.

He hoped she'd be pleased.

Chapter Ten

Wade hardly slept on Sunday night and by Monday morning, he was filled with nervous energy as he faced his first teaching job. He'd spoken to Valerie several times over the weekend to let her know he would fill the position, and then to find out what he needed to do to get the special license. She told him what his responsibilities would be, and he had spent hours researching online before making his first lesson plan. His students would range in age from five to fourteen, which was a large gap. But his biggest priority would be the Christmas program.

"Our class has music on Monday mornings," Issy said as they drove toward the school. "So, I'll see you today, Daddy."

"I'm not sure if it's reassuring that you'll be one of my first classes—or if it's intimidating, Bug."

She grinned at him in the rearview mirror. "You're going to do great!"

"Thanks for the confidence boost."

They pulled into the parking lot, and he was relieved to see Valerie's car already there. It was just after seven, but he wanted to give himself enough time to get settled into his classroom. He and Valerie had visited it on Sunday, after church, so he had a good feel for what he had to work with and what he might need to bring from home.

After parking, he and the kids got out of his truck and walked into the school. It had snowed the night before and there was a fresh coat on all the surfaces. Someone had already shoveled the walkways and plowed the parking lot, for which Wade was thankful.

"Will we come to the music room before school starts?" Issy asked Wade.

"That's the plan. You can go to your classrooms before the first bell rings."

Valerie was just walking out of her office when they entered the school.

"Perfect timing," she said with a smile. She was wearing a pair of black pants, a white button-down shirt and a gray jacket. She always looked put together and professional. Wade usually wore Carhartt pants and a flannel shirt to work—but today, he was wearing slacks and a simple button-down shirt. He had gone back and forth about wearing a tie but had decided it was a little too dressy for him. "I was just coming to look for you," she said.

"Oh?"

"I thought we could go over Mrs. Cole's Christmas program before the first-class period. She told me where I could find the file."

"Great."

Hailey stepped out of Valerie's office and

she and Issy linked arms as they talked quietly. The little group walked down the long hallway to the end of the building where the music room and the art room were located.

Wade had a set of keys for the room, so he slipped one into the lock and opened the door for everyone to enter.

Issy and Hailey sat on a pair of chairs as Hailey opened her backpack and pulled out their friendship bracelet supplies. Brayden went to the music closet where all the instruments were located and pulled out a xylophone to play with.

"Mrs. Cole said her Christmas program folder is in the top drawer of her filing cabinet," Valerie said as she walked across the room.

Wade followed. The teacher's desk was in the farthest corner, and it was exactly as Mrs. Cole had left it on Wednesday when she'd gone home for Thanksgiving break. A picture of her family, complete with her grandchildren, sat on one side, while a calendar and miscellaneous supplies sat on the other side. It was a tidy little office space and when Valerie opened the filing cabinet, she found what she was looking for.

"Have a seat," Wade said as he pointed to the desk chair. He pulled a stool over to join her as she spread the file open.

Wade set his shoulder bag on the floor next to the desk and took off his coat to set on top before he took a seat on the stool.

"Hmm," Valerie said as she looked over the papers in the file.

"Is that good or bad?" he asked.

She let out a sigh. "It looks like these are the notes she kept from the past few years with the titles of the songs they sang, and the scriptures recited. She has a list of who played which part in the nativity— but that's all. She doesn't have anything laid out for this year. At least, not that I can see."

"She didn't already select the songs or give out the parts?"

Valerie shook her head. "I don't see anything like that. Maybe there's another file."

She stood and opened the top drawer, then looked through several files before closing it and opening the second drawer. When she had gone through the entire cabinet, she turned back to Wade and shrugged. "I can't find anything."

"Should we call her?"

"It's kind of early, but we can give it a try."

Valerie pulled her cell phone out of her back pocket and took a seat again. She found Mrs. Cole's number and pressed the talk icon and then put the call on speakerphone.

It didn't take long for Mrs. Cole to answer. "Hello, Miss Wilmington. How can I help you?"

"Hello, Mrs. Cole. I'm here with Mr. Griffin, who will be subbing for you this coming month."

"Hello, Mr. Griffin," Mrs. Cole said. "Thank you so much for stepping in to help. I don't know what we would do without you."

"I'm happy to help," he said.

"Good."

"Mrs. Cole," Valerie continued, "we found the file that you told me about, with notes about the past few pageants. But I'm not finding anything about this year's program. Do you have that available?"

"Oh, dear. I thought I explained. I was going to put the program together this weekend, over the Thanksgiving break, but I didn't get a chance. I only have the notes from years past." A child began to cry in the background. Mrs. Cole paused for a second and addressed the child's problem before returning her attention to the conversation. "I'm so sorry. I'm alone with the kids right now, since my husband is at the grocery store. My son-in-law is at work and my daughter is at the hospital with the new baby."

"How is the baby doing?" Valerie asked.

"We're taking things one day at a time.

Yesterday, there were some complications and they struggled to keep the baby's body temperature up. But it seems she's turned a new leaf and things are looking better today."

"I'm happy to hear that," Valerie said.

"I'm sorry—I didn't mean to get side-tracked," Mrs. Cole said. "There's just so much going on here." The child continued to cry in the background. "Would you like me to put the program together and email it to you?"

"Oh, no," Valerie said. "Don't worry about a thing. Mr. Griffin and I will put the program together this year. You focus on your family. I just wanted to make sure I wasn't missing something important."

"I'm so sorry," Mrs. Cole said. "I feel like I'm leaving you in a pinch."

"Don't even think about it," Valerie assured her. "We've got things under control."

"Okay. I should run. Call or text me if you need anything else."

"We will. Goodbye." Valerie hung up the phone and turned to Wade, an apology on her face. "I'm sorry, Wade."

"It's not your fault. We'll figure it out. How hard can it be to choose a few songs and assign the parts of the nativity play?"

"You don't know all the students, nor what they are or are not capable of," she said.

He hadn't thought about that.

"I know all of them," Valerie said, "but I don't know their musical abilities. I could probably take a good stab at it and try to come up with a cast list."

"I'm happy to help," he assured her. "I know a few of the kids. And I can try to get a feel today with the classes that I have."

Valerie nodded. "I think that's a good idea." She glanced at the clock. "We won't have enough time during school. Why don't you and the kids come over for supper tonight and we can put the program together?"

"Are you sure?"

"Of course." She smiled at him, her eyes softening. "Having supper together is starting to become a habit."

He returned her smile. "It's a habit I'm enjoying quite a bit."

Her cheeks blossomed with color and her dimples shone. He could get used to looking for those dimples.

"At least let me bring something," he said.

She waved his offer away. "I have a roast with vegetables in the slow cooker, and Hailey and I made some fresh bread yesterday after church. We have some leftover pies that need to get eaten, so we'll have plenty of food."

"I'm kind of relieved at the offer. With everything going on this weekend and trying to get all my plans in order this morning, I haven't thought ahead to supper, and I need to get to the grocery store, which might not happen today. Supper at your house sounds great."

"Then it's settled. Come over about five and we'll have supper and then sit down with Mrs. Cole's notes and come up with a plan. For now, perhaps focus on "Silent Night." Mrs. Cole said she always ends the program with the students circling the sanctuary with battery-operated candles, singing that song."

"That I do remember," Wade said.

She studied him for a second and then said, "You're going to do a wonderful job, Wade."

"Thank you." With her reassurance, he felt like maybe he would.

"I need to do a couple of things before the first bell," she told him as she closed the file folder and stood. "But I'll be back when the first class comes in at 9:10—I think it's Hailey and Issy's class, if I'm not mistaken. I'll let the students know what's happened to Mrs. Cole and introduce them to you. Will that be okay?"

"Sure. I'll be happy to see you whenever you want to stop by." He was flirting with her—he couldn't seem to help it. But it suddenly occurred to him that Valerie was his boss and he needed to keep things professional. At least during school hours.

She just smiled at him and then called for Hailey.

"Can't I wait in here with Issy until school starts?" Hailey asked.

"Do you mind, Wade?" Valerie asked, turning to him.

"Not at all. I'll send them off before the bell rings."

"Thanks. I'll see you later." She left the music room and Wade moved the stool aside so he could sit at the desk.

He had a lot to prepare before the first class arrived—but his excitement was starting to outweigh his nerves. Already, this was more appealing to him than working construction—especially in the winter.

Hopefully he felt the same by the end of the day.

Valerie loved the smell of roasting meat and vegetables that permeated her house.

It gave her a warm, homey feeling. Hailey was at the dining-room table finishing her homework with Annabelle on her lap, and Valerie was in the kitchen putting together an oatmeal spice cake, which she would pop into the oven. It would add another aroma to the air, and even though they had enough dessert with the leftover pies, she loved a good oatmeal spice cake after eating a roast.

It was almost five and Valerie was eager for Wade and the kids to arrive. She'd seen him several times at school that day and each time their paths had crossed, her heart had done a little flip. It had been the highlight of her week—and it had only just begun. She was excited to see him tomorrow and the day after that and the day after that.

But they hadn't had a lot of time to talk about how his classes had gone. She'd been caught up in a meeting with the school board at the end of the day and so she was looking forward to hearing about it when they got to her house.

"Can you help me?" Hailey asked from the dining room in a whiny voice.

"I'm happy to help as soon as I get this in the oven," Valerie said as she opened the oven door and slipped the glass cake pan inside. She set the timer and then walked into the dining room. "What are you working on?"

"Decimal points." Hailey made a face. "I hate math."

"Hate is a strong word, Hailey. I didn't like it when I was your age, either. But once I realized that math was simply a set of rules, and if I learned them and followed them, I could do any math problem I was given, I didn't dislike it so much."

Hailey scrunched up her nose as if Valerie didn't know what she was talking about.

Valerie sat next to Hailey at the table and had the little girl show her the problem.

"Okay," Valerie said as she realized

what she was working on. "Let's look at it this way." She laid out the problem in a real-world situation and walked Hailey through, step-by-step.

When they were done, Hailey grinned up at Valerie. "That wasn't so hard."

"See," Valerie said, touching Hailey's chin. "I told you. Now do the next one."

Hailey bit her tongue as she worked on the next math problem, and when she came up with the correct answer, she cheered.

Valerie sat back, marveling at her daughter. Sometimes, it took her off guard that this was her child. Hailey was a part of her—a big part of her—and she loved sharing her life with her.

The front doorbell rang, and Valerie stood.

"Can I finish the last problem later?" Hailey asked Valerie.

"Sure."

They walked through the living room and Hailey pulled the door open. Like usual, there was the excited round of greetings, with Annabelle included. Wade looked tired, but happy to see Valerie.

"Come in," she said as she helped the kids hang up their coats. "Supper will be ready in about twenty minutes," she told them as they ran up the stairs toward Hailey's bedroom.

Wade took off his coat as Valerie closed the door behind him.

"You look tired," she said.

"I'm exhausted. I don't care what anyone says. An eight-hour day in construction is nothing compared to an eight-hour day with students. And I only had three classes today. I don't know what I'll do with four."

She put her hand on his arm and gave it a gentle squeeze. "You'll do great. All the teachers who had students in your class today told me how much the kids enjoyed themselves. They said you were funny and nice, and they want to go back to music class tomorrow."

His muscle tensed under her hand as he

put his hand over hers. It was warm and gentle, and she suddenly found herself wondering what it would feel like to have his arms around her—a thought that startled her and made her pull away from him.

More and more, Valerie found herself daydreaming about Wade Griffin. Her feelings for him were growing faster than she liked to admit. Yet the more time she spent with him, the more time she wanted to spend with him.

"Thank you," he said, showing no sign that he noticed her sudden apprehension. "That's nice to hear."

"Come in," she said as she moved toward the dining room. "I could use some help setting the table. And I want to hear all about your day."

They worked in tandem, and Valerie marveled that Wade was comfortable enough in her home to know where to find the plates, cups, silverware and napkins without asking or being told. They visited as if they'd known each other for years—instead of just a few months.

Wade's stories about his first day of teaching made her laugh. It was fun to share this part of her life with him. To work with the same people, know the same students and commiserate about the coffee in the teachers' lounge. Wade teased her that everyone blamed the coffee on her, but they all knew it was the secretary, Mrs. Freeman, who purchased the coffee and insisted on that brand.

They didn't even get around to talking about the Christmas program before supper. Instead, they talked about Thanksgiving break and when the conversation shifted to his parents' unexpected visit, he told her about his childhood growing up in Timber Falls. He had one older sister who lived in Oregon and only came home at Christmas. They talked about Wade's need to come home and work for his dad after his divorce. Neither one noticed that half an hour had passed until the timer went off on the oven and the cake was ready to come out.

"We should get the kids down here to eat," Valerie said.

"I'll call them."

As Wade left to tell the kids to come to supper, Valerie pulled the cake out of the oven. She had a cream cheese frosting ready to put on it, but it would need to cool first.

When everyone was seated, Valerie asked Wade if he'd like to offer grace.

He met her gaze and for a second, she held her breath.

This was starting to feel an awful lot like a family.

And she liked it—was beginning to love it.

"Of course," he said.

They held hands as Wade said grace and then they began to eat the meal.

The kids were just as comfortable with each other as Wade and Valerie had become and they laughed and visited as the meal progressed.

When everyone was done, the kids began to clear the table and Wade and Valerie hand-washed the dishes. He flicked some suds at her, and she laughed as she retaliated.

The kids asked to watch a movie in Valerie's bedroom and after they were settled, Valerie came downstairs and found Wade at the table with a pad of paper and a pen.

"Ready to plan the best Christmas pageant ever?" he asked.

She took the seat next to him, trying not to be aware of their nearness, or the subtle scent of his cologne—or her desire to touch him. To feel his skin against hers—to know what it would be like in his arms. To be kissed again.

She forced herself to focus on the task ahead—but it was almost impossible. She loved having him in her home—in her life.

Was Wade feeling what she was feeling? Or was this one-sided? She'd told him they needed to remain friends, but could she stick to that plan? Had she ruined things by telling him that's what she wanted, when she was starting to change her mind?

He turned to her, a question in his beautiful blue eyes. They were so clear. So honest. So kind. She could get lost in those eyes.

"Everything okay?" he asked quietly.

She couldn't speak, so she simply nodded.

He studied her for another heartbeat and then tore his gaze away from hers and cleared his throat. "I think we should start with the play." His voice sounded a little strained—but was she only imagining that?

"Okay," she managed to say.

"Do you think we could cast Hailey to play the part of Mary?" he asked. "When she was singing today, I was really impressed with her vocal ability. And she has so much confidence. Since she's new to the school, I also thought it might be good for her to feel ownership of the play. Other kids would get to know her better and she might feel like she has a place here."

Unexpected tears came to Valerie's eyes. "Really? You want her to play Mary?"

He looked at her again. "If you think she'd enjoy it."

"I think she'd love it." She wanted to hug him—but she refrained, knowing that if they went down that road, there was no coming back without pain.

And pain was the last thing she wanted for her—or for Hailey.

"Great," he said as he wrote Hailey's name on the list.

They worked for over an hour on their Christmas pageant plan, brainstorming ideas, and going over Mrs. Cole's notes.

Valerie found herself laughing again as Wade told her stories about the previous pageants and some of the foibles that had taken place. A wise man who had the hiccups, a sheep who loved the limelight and spent the entire program bleating, though he was repeatedly told to stop, and the various singers who tried to out-sing each other to be heard above the noise.

When they were finished, and both were satisfied with the plan, Valerie cut some cake and they each enjoyed a piece before calling the children down to join them.

"I think this year will be a memorable year, if nothing else," Wade said as he took a bite of his cake.

"For all the right reasons," she said as she savored the spices on her tongue.

"Mmm." He looked down at his cake. "This is so good, Valerie."

"Thank you."

"Your cooking and baking have spoiled the kids and me. We might need to do this more often."

She didn't meet his gaze as she said, "Part of me wants to tell you that we should make a habit of it."

He was silent for a moment and then said, "And the other part?"

"The other part is scared and making a list of all the reasons it wouldn't be a good idea." She finally looked up at him.

Wade was watching her, and she could see that he was struggling, too. "I think you and I are telling ourselves the same things."

She felt a sense of relief to finally be voicing what she'd been feeling for several days—and to know he was on the same page.

"I like you, Valerie," he said. "A lot."

"I like you, too," she said quietly.

"But I think both of us know what we're up against. The least of which is that I'm now your employee and I have a feeling there's some kind of policy against dating your boss."

A smile tilted the edges of her lips. "If there is, I haven't seen one. But I know what you mean." Sadness filled her heart as she played with the crumbs of her cake. "My life drastically changed less than two weeks ago—I think that's about all the change I can handle for a while."

He was silent again as he, too, pushed his cake around with his fork. When he looked up at her, he offered a sad smile. "I'm thankful for your friendship, Valerie. More than I can say."

"So am I." And she was—very much—but was it enough?

It would have to be.

Chapter Eleven

Snow was falling thick outside Valerie's bedroom window as she touched up her makeup in the mirror. It was dark outside, and her bedroom lamp offered a warm glow as she applied a little more lipstick.

"We're going to be late, kids," Valerie called as she set the lipstick aside and touched her hair to smooth down a few wayward strands. "We need to get going."

"It's just dress rehearsal," Hailey called back from the adjoining bedroom.

"Dress rehearsal is the most important of all the rehearsals," Valerie said as she turned off the light and walked into Hailey's bedroom.

Hailey and Issy were sitting on Hailey's bed, while Brayden was on the floor with Annabelle. Whenever Valerie needed to look for Brayden, she always looked for Annabelle.

"Are you three ready?" Valerie asked. "Your dad is expecting us at the school in less than ten minutes. And with all the snow that fell this afternoon, the roads probably aren't plowed. It'll take us some time to get there."

"Do we have to go?" Brayden asked with a frown. "I'm just a silly shepherd. I don't have any lines and it's boring to sit there."

"Sorry, buddy," Valerie said. "Everyone has to be there tonight."

He sighed and pulled himself off the floor.

Valerie had taken the kids home after school while Wade had stayed behind to work with the sound technicians on microphones and music. She had fed the kids supper and then helped the girls put on a little bit of stage makeup. It was time to get back for dress rehearsal. She had been helping Wade with rehearsals for the past four weeks, but she hadn't been at all of them, and she was eager to see how everything had come together.

They trooped downstairs and Brayden put Annabelle in her crate as the girls put on their coats. Over the past four weeks, they had all spent a lot of time together. Valerie made supper for them at least once a week on the nights that Wade worked late on the pageant. There were several times that they stayed later after school to build the set and repair the costumes.

But Valerie had enjoyed every moment of it. Ever since Wade had been at her house for supper, and they had admitted that they both wanted more, the tension and chemistry had grown between them. Though neither one made a move in that direction.

She didn't want to think about what

would happen when the Christmas pageant was over, and they didn't have any reason for spending so much time together. Would they make a reason?

The snow was still falling and had piled up along Valerie's sidewalk. She took the shovel and pushed it out of the way so they could get to the car. The snow was light and fluffy, making it easy to shovel, and they were soon on the road toward school.

Christmas lights decorated many of the houses in her neighborhood and the kids oohed and aahed over them as they drove. Downtown, lighted wreaths hung from the historic streetlamps and several of the businesses were still open, welcoming Christmas shoppers.

"Only five days to Christmas!" Issy said from the back seat.

"We made a paper chain in our classroom," Brayden piped up. "Five circles left to pull off."

"Tomorrow's the last day of classes," Hailey added—as if Valerie hadn't been counting down the days to Christmas break herself.

"Are you excited for the pageant tomorrow night?" Valerie asked them as she turned onto Broadway, driving slowly in the snow.

"Yes!" came a chorus of answers.

"I'm excited for it to be done," Brayden said.

Valerie smiled and kept her response to herself. Brayden hadn't been a fan of the pageant from the beginning and liked to remind everyone whenever he could.

They pulled into the back parking lot, which the school shared with the church. The school program would be held in the church sanctuary. Tomorrow would be Friday, so they would have to take down the entire set after the pageant to get the space ready for Sunday-morning service.

Valerie had never been so excited for the Christmas season. She always enjoyed the holidays, but things were so much different with children in the house. There were already presents under the tree, with more coming on Christmas morning. She and the kids had spent several evenings baking cookies, and Hailey's sweet voice had filled the house with the sound of carols every day. Even Annabelle was sporting a Christmas sweater that Hailey had insisted they buy for the little white dog.

And tomorrow night, her daughter would play Mary in the school's highly anticipated Christmas pageant. Every time she thought about it, her chest filled with something like pride. But not boastful pride—it was a humble, awe-inspiring feeling to know that this little girl was her daughter. Of all the children in the world—this one was hers.

She just wished Hailey would let her tell people the truth.

Especially Wade.

She was pleased to see that someone had plowed the parking lot. Since the snow was still falling, they would need to plow it again, but at least it was semi-clear for now.

Everyone left the car and bustled into the warm building. There were several families already inside, waiting for the rehearsal to begin.

Valerie said hello to a few of them and helped the kids take off their coats and hang them on the hooks in the back entrance of the church sanctuary.

She could hear Wade's voice above the din of others, and she smiled.

"Come into the sanctuary after you hang up your coats," he was telling everyone. "We need to get going as soon as possible."

He came around the corner and his gaze caught on her, and he smiled.

It wasn't just any smile—it was the smile of familiarity, happiness and tenderness. A smile that two people who cared for each other shared.

She returned the smile, loving to see him in this environment. He was thriving as a music teacher. His eyes shone every time he walked into the Timber Falls Christian School, and whenever she saw him with his students, he had the same look of genuine happiness. Like he had found his purpose.

And, perhaps, he had.

It was fun to watch him thrive.

"Come on," she told the three kids. "Let's get into the sanctuary."

The kids found their friends and ran to find their seats as Valerie joined Wade just outside the sanctuary doors.

"How did the sound check go?" she asked him.

"Great. One of the microphones isn't working like it should, but hopefully we can get that figured out by tomorrow. Thanks again for taking the kids home with you. I don't know what I'd do without your help."

"I promised I'd help you," she said.

"You did—and you upheld your promise well."

"There's still one day to go," she teased.

He only had eyes for her as he said, "I

know you'll be just as wonderful tomorrow as you were the last four weeks."

She felt her cheeks blushing—something that Wade seemed to make a common occurrence.

As everyone entered the sanctuary around them, Valerie felt like it was just the two of them standing there together.

"What will we do after the pageant is over?" she asked him.

"Rest?" he chuckled.

She wanted to clarify that she meant how would they find reasons to see each other outside of school, but now wasn't the time or place. And, the truth was, she wasn't sure if Wade would still want to be friends—or more—once he learned the truth about Hailey. They'd spent over a month together and she'd never told him that Hailey was her daughter. He'd be hurt and confused—but she hoped he wouldn't be mad.

"When everything is done," Valerie said,

"we'll need to talk about what's happening after Christmas break."

"What's happening?" he asked, a slight frown on his face—though there was also something like anticipation. "With us?"

"No," she said quickly, the heat moving from her cheeks to her neck. "I mean, with your job as a substitute teacher."

"Oh." He sounded disappointed—but rallied. "Have you spoken to Mrs. Cole?"

"Just this morning. She said that the new baby is doing well, but they don't anticipate that she'll be able to leave the hospital until early February, which would have been her original due date. Mrs. Cole would like to stay in Oklahoma until then to help." Valerie paused, not knowing if this was the time or place to tell him the rest—though it needed to be said. "She actually told me that she might not be coming back."

Wade frowned as he gently took Valerie's hand and led her to the corner of the room for a little more privacy.

"What?" he asked.

She loved the feel of his hand—and when he let her go, she wanted to take it back. But she couldn't. Not here, in front of these people—and not before she told him the truth about Hailey. Nothing could happen until then.

"This was her last year teaching. I knew that much—but I thought I would have the summer to find a replacement. She's thinking about taking the rest of the year off and staying in Oklahoma to help her daughter once the baby comes home from the hospital. She asked me to look for a permanent replacement."

His blue eyes were intent as he studied her. "What does that mean?"

"It means that the job is yours for the rest of the year if you'd like it. But, if you want to continue in a permanent position, you'll need to work on getting a teaching certificate. You'll need to officially apply for the job when it comes available and go through the whole process. But I can tell you that the school board has been very happy with your work this past month and we've been getting great reports from students and teachers. I don't see any reason the school board would deny you a permanent position—if you want one."

"Wow." He pulled back—just a bit—and frowned. "That's a big decision to make."

"It's very big," she agreed. "But you don't need to make it now. You have a lot of time to decide. If you decide to go for it, I recommend starting the process to get your teaching certificate as soon as possible, though."

He nodded slowly and took a deep breath.

"I'm sorry," she said. "I didn't know when to tell you. I know you have a lot on your mind with the pageant right now. I shouldn't have said anything yet."

"It's okay." He returned his focus to her, his expression softening. "I'm happy you told me. I'll need to take everything into consideration, and the more time I have, the better. Thank you for telling me."

"I love how you always put my mind at ease, Wade. Even when you're the one who has to make a tough decision."

"I want you to be happy, Valerie. I like when I'm the one who can make you happy."

Her heart beat hard at the look in his eyes, and she tried not to get emotional. "Thank you."

He gently touched her hand and then said, "I should get this rehearsal started. We can talk later."

"Okay." She nodded as they joined the stream of kids and parents entering the sanctuary.

She couldn't wait for later.

Wade felt both proud and frustrated as the pageant dress rehearsal commenced. Some of the kids were very serious and had all their lines memorized. Some, like Brayden, wanted to be anywhere else but in that sanctuary—in their costumes.

"This is when the shepherds and sheep

enter," Wade called to the little boys and girls offstage who had been chosen for these roles. "The angels should be ready on stage right to come in and sing about the birth of Jesus for the shepherds to hear."

Valerie stood on stage left with the shepherds and the sheep while another parent volunteer was on stage right.

The shepherds and sheep entered the stage, some of them excited—others bored—and took their places.

"Brayden," Wade warned as he saw a look in his son's eyes, "keep your staff to yourself. No one should be using their staffs as lightsabers or swords."

Brayden pressed his lips together in a frown and sighed.

The sheep and shepherds were the youngest cast members and it felt chaotic as they roamed about the stage.

"Everyone needs to find one place and sit down," Wade told them. "There's no need to move."

They did as instructed, though a few of them seemed lost in their own daydreams.

"All right," Wade called, "angels, it's time to enter and start singing 'While Shepherds Watched Their Flocks.'"

The older students who played the angels entered and lined up on the risers, their hands in the praying position, as they sang their song beautifully.

Wade breathed a sigh of relief—but then he noticed that the boy playing Joseph was having a thumb war with Hailey, who was playing Mary—and he walked over to them on the side of the stage.

Valerie must have noticed, too, because she joined him at the same time—but she nodded at Wade to continue.

Wade squatted down in front of the manger where the doll was lying and whispered, "I need both of you to behave as you will tomorrow during the performance. I don't think Mary and Joseph were playing thumb war the night Jesus was born—do you?"

Ryan Asher, the boy playing Joseph, sighed. "What *did* Joseph do in the manger? Mary had the baby, the wise men gave gifts, the angels sang—what did *he* do?"

"Joseph had one of the most important jobs in the world," Wade said. "He was there to comfort and protect Mary and the baby Jesus."

Ryan lifted his chin with excitement. "Like a warrior?"

"Exactly."

Wade stood and moved away from the nativity—but he caught Valerie's gaze and the look he saw there took his breath away.

There were tears in her eyes as she leaned close and whispered in his ear, "That was the most beautiful thing I've ever heard."

They stood close to each other as they watched the rest of the scene unfold. His hand brushed hers, but she didn't pull away, and his chest tightened with all the love and emotions he felt toward her.

Because somewhere along the way, when

he'd least expected it, he'd fallen in love with Valerie Wilmington. He marveled at that fact, thinking about the first time he'd met her when she'd come to Timber Falls Christian School. He'd assumed she was cold and rigid—but he'd been wrong. So wrong.

He was soon needed as the wise men began their journey toward Bethlehem from the back of the sanctuary.

His thoughts were with Valerie, though, and all the things he wanted to tell her. He was trying not to think about what she'd said earlier about the job opening up, and being permanent. His heart told him it was what he wanted—but his head wasn't in agreement. It was a huge risk. He'd have to leave the family business permanently— yet he knew his dad was hoping he'd take over the business someday.

Wade was finally using his talents and skills and he felt like he was alive. Really alive.

It didn't hurt that Valerie was there every

day either. Even if she wasn't, he loved what he was doing.

There would be time to think about that later, so he pushed his thoughts away and focused on the dress rehearsal.

It wasn't perfect, but the kids knew where they belonged and had their lines and the songs memorized. At eight, it was time to wrap things up, so Wade gave them last minute instructions about when to be at the school tomorrow evening. He'd see several of them in class tomorrow, though he didn't want to bog down their last day before Christmas break with more instructions. Instead, he'd use the time for some fun holiday games and treats.

"I'll see all of you tomorrow," Wade called to them. "Get a good night's sleep!"

"Goodbye, Mr. Griffin," several of the students called as they left the sanctuary to join their waiting parents.

The space slowly emptied, and since Wade had the keys to the building, he would be the last to leave.

Valerie and Hailey stayed behind to help

straighten up the set and organize the costumes in the two Sunday school classrooms where the boys and girls would get dressed tomorrow.

When everything was ready, and the kids and Valerie were in their coats by the back door, Wade turned off all the lights and they walked out into the parking lot. He had already used his remote start to turn on the truck, so Issy and Brayden said good-night to Hailey and ran off to wait in the truck. Hailey did the same with Valerie's car, which was also running and warm.

Wade locked the back door as Valerie waited by his side. The church Christmas lights offered a soft glow on the snow and allowed him to see the lock.

The snow was still falling and when Wade turned away from the door, he caught Valerie looking up into the dark sky, a gentle smile on her face.

"It never gets old, does it?" he asked.

"What?" She pulled her gaze away from the sky.

"Falling snow. The cold is hard, and the winter starts to feel long in January, but each snowfall feels like a miracle—especially before Christmas."

"You were wonderful in there tonight," Valerie said. "You're always wonderful, Wade. I love how you look at the world. As if there's always something good to be found."

"There is always something good," he said quietly. "I see it in you all the time."

They were standing close, and he wanted to pull her into his arms, to show her how much he cared for her. He had never felt this way about anyone—not even Amber. Their relationship had been tumultuous from the beginning. Exciting in a different kind of way. With Valerie, it was mature, grown-up, comforting and hopeful. There was nothing tumultuous about their relationship. Everything with Valerie felt steady, secure and exciting because it was promising.

The snowflakes were cold as they landed on his face and then melted. They collected on Valerie's dark hat and on her eye-lashes, and when one landed on her cheek, he wanted to kiss it away.

His breath came hard as he stared at her.

"Will you come over after the pageant tomorrow night?" she asked him, her gaze hopeful—yet cautious. "We can celebrate the success of your first school program and the beginning of the Christmas holi-day break."

It was the first time she'd invited him and the kids over without a reason—at least, a real reason. The first time was because Issy was at her house, the sec-ond time was because he was working on the tree house. The time after that was to plan the Christmas program. And each time after that was because she was help-ing him with the pageant.

This time, she was inviting him because she wanted to spend time with him. And that changed everything.

"We'll come," he said as he took a step closer to her to wipe the melted snowflake from her cheek, "but then you'll need to let us reciprocate and have you over for Christmas Eve dinner."

She was still beneath his touch. She did not back up, or shy away, but smiled.

"We would love to join you for Christmas Eve."

"Just because," he whispered.

"Just because," she agreed.

His truck's remote start turned off and he knew the vehicle would get cold quickly. Besides, his kids were watching, and he didn't want to do anything that might cause a lot of questions—at least, not yet.

He was in love with Valerie, but there were a lot of things they needed to work out before he could tell her. The most important was that she still didn't trust him with the truth about her past—or why her mother had brought Hailey to live with her unexpectedly. Every time he tried to broach the subject, she shied away from telling him what had happened. He wasn't sure why she didn't trust him with the information, but he wanted her to trust him.

And, until she did, he didn't think it was wise to tell her how he was feeling.

It was enough to know that she wanted him to be part of her life.

But, one day soon, he hoped to be so much more.

"Good night, Valerie." He leaned forward and kissed her forehead, leaving his lips there for longer than necessary.

She pressed against him, putting her hands on the lapel of his coat.

When he pulled away, she looked up at him and he saw the invitation in her eyes to kiss her—truly kiss her—but he hesitated. He didn't want anything between them when he kissed her for the first time—and he didn't want an audience.

"Good night," he said.

"Good night."

They walked to their vehicles and shared one more look before he pulled out of the parking lot.

"Daddy likes Miss Wilmington," Issy said in a singsong voice from the back seat. "Does she like you, Daddy?"

He smiled to himself, a little embarrassed that his daughter had witnessed his moment with Valerie. "I think so—I hope so."

"I think she does," Issy said.

Wade drove home through the falling snow, feeling like his life was finally heading toward a destination of his choosing. One he wasn't forced to take because of life circumstances, or unplanned events. He was doing a job he loved, and he was falling for a woman who was nothing like his first wife. She encouraged him to step outside of his comfort zone and was there to help him every step of the way.

He wasn't falling for Valerie.

He had fallen.

Chapter Twelve

Valerie followed Wade out of the parking lot and when he turned right onto Broadway and she turned left, she felt herself being torn. Part of her wanted to be in that truck with him, heading to a home they shared, putting the kids to bed and then enjoying a quiet evening together. He was the last thing she thought about before going to bed and the first thing she thought about when she woke up. She looked for him all day at school and had loved spending the extra time with him, working on the Christmas pageant.

She hated saying goodbye to him.

"Do you like Issy's dad?" Hailey asked from the back seat. "Did he kiss you?"

"He kissed my forehead," she said.

"That means he kissed you." Hailey sighed, and when Valerie looked in the rearview mirror as they passed under a streetlamp, she saw that her daughter was smiling.

Valerie hadn't forgotten what Hailey said about wanting a dad. It was one of the many things that had been denied her daughter.

Yet—Valerie couldn't even contemplate dating Wade if he didn't know the truth about her and Hailey. It was already beyond the point of bringing up casually. Valerie would need to be very intentional about telling him and telling him in a way that made him realize why she had waited.

But she wanted Hailey's permission to tell their secret. It wasn't just Valerie's to tell. Was Hailey ready to let people know the truth?

They drove through the quiet streets and

into the alley behind Valerie's house. After parking her car, they walked through the newly fallen snow to the back door and let themselves into the kitchen.

"I'll let Annabelle out while you get on your pajamas and brush your teeth," Valerie told her daughter as she flipped on a light. "I'll be up in a bit to pray with you and tuck you in."

Hailey was about to take off her coat when she surprised Valerie and wrapped her arms around Valerie's waist in a tight hug.

Valerie paused and then she returned the hug, their winter coats making it a little awkward—but she didn't mind. Tears came to her eyes as Hailey held her close.

"What's this about?" Valerie asked.

Hailey pulled back and looked up at her. "I just wanted to hug you."

"Okay." She smiled. "You can hug me whenever you want."

"I know." Hailey wrapped her arms

around her again. "Thank you for taking such good care of me."

The tears fell from Valerie's eyes as she reached down and picked Hailey up, hugging her tight as Hailey's feet dangled. They had talked to her mom twice since Thanksgiving, and both times, Hailey had told her all the fun and exciting things taking place in her life. At the end of both conversations, though, Hailey had told her mom how much she missed her and how she wanted things to go back to the way they once were. It had broken Valerie's heart, because she had thought they were making progress.

This hug was the first real indication that perhaps Hailey had accepted her.

"You're welcome," Valerie said as she sniffed back tears, burying her face into Hailey's hair.

"Are you crying?" Hailey asked.

"Yes."

"Why?"

"Because I love you."

Hailey pulled back and looked at Valerie, eye to eye. "I love you and I'm not crying."

"You love me?" Valerie asked.

Her daughter nodded—and then smiled.

"Oh, Hailey." Valerie hugged her close again. "You don't know how happy that makes me."

"Are you still crying?" Hailey asked.

"Yes. Because I'm so happy."

Hailey wrapped her arms around Valerie's neck and held her close. "You don't need to cry."

Annabelle began to whimper from her crate, so Valerie set Hailey down. She wiped her cheeks as she said, "Run up and get ready for bed. I'll be up soon."

Hailey did as she was instructed, and Valerie let out Annabelle. As the small dog stepped tentatively through the new snow, Valerie stood at the back door and marveled at Hailey's words.

Her daughter loved her. It wasn't something that she would take for granted. She had never assumed Hailey loved her just because she was her daughter. But, to hear the words from Hailey's mouth meant everything.

Joy filled Valerie's heart at the knowledge—and at the tenderness Wade had shown her before they left the church. Could it be that Valerie could have everything her heart longed for? A husband, a family, a career and a home?

"Come on, Annabelle," Valerie called to her dog as the cold began to bother her.

Annabelle scampered inside and immediately left the kitchen, no doubt in search of Hailey.

After Valerie took off her outdoor gear and locked all the doors, she turned off the lights and stopped for a second near the Christmas tree in the living room. They had left the lights on the tree while they'd been away, and they needed to be turned off now.

She admired them for a minute and then unplugged the cord before heading up the stairs to get ready for bed.

Hailey was already in bed, under the covers, with Annabelle by her side. Her lights were still on since Valerie usually turned them off when it was time to sleep. Hailey was reading a book she had borrowed from the library. Since the school shared a backyard with the public library, the school hadn't put in a library of their own. They simply took the classes to the public library once a week to check out books.

"Did you brush your teeth?" Valerie asked Hailey.

Hailey responded by giving her a big, toothy grin.

"Good." Valerie picked up the clothes Hailey had been wearing and put them in the wicker basket. "You know I like your room to be tidy. Please don't leave your dirty clothes on the floor."

"I forgot," Hailey said with a shrug.

Valerie switched on the lamp by Hailey's bed and then turned off the overhead light. She took a seat on the side of

Hailey's bed and asked, "Are you excited about the Christmas program?"

"Yes."

"Are you nervous?"

"A little."

"It's normal to be nervous."

"I know. Mr. Griffin told us that. He said that the nerves help us to stay alert and be ready to do our parts."

"That's very true. Nerves help us to care about what we're doing. If we didn't care, we wouldn't try our hardest to do the best we can do." Valerie wanted to shift the conversation to a different topic. She wanted to talk to Hailey about sharing the truth with Wade and Issy. But was it too soon after she had told Valerie she loved her? Would Hailey get resentful? Or was it the perfect opportunity?

There was only one way to find out.

"I asked Wade if he and the kids would like to come over tomorrow after the pageant," she said tentatively.

Hailey's eyes lit up with excitement. "Can we bake cookies again?"

"Maybe not tomorrow night. We'll be busy all day and then it'll be a little late when they come over. But we can bake cookies another day soon. Tomorrow is the last day of school before Christmas break."

"Yay!" she said. "Can Issy have a sleep-over?"

The girls had been begging for weeks. Maybe now would be a good time. "I'll ask Wade and see what he thinks."

"Okay." Hailey grinned as she eagerly petted Annabelle and gave the dog a kiss.

"There's something else I'd like to discuss," Valerie continued.

Hailey watched her closely but didn't speak.

"I think it's time we tell Issy and her dad that I'm your real mom."

"Why?"

"Because we've become very good friends and—" She paused, not knowing how to continue. "I like Wade a lot, Hailey. And I would like to spend more time with him, but I feel like I'm keeping a secret from him, and I don't like that feeling. You wouldn't like if Issy and her dad were keeping a secret from us, would you?"

Hailey continued to pet Annabelle and Valerie could see that she was deep in thought.

"I think tomorrow would be a good time," Valerie said. "After the Christmas pageant, when they come to our house. What do you think? We don't have to tell everyone—yet—but I think it's important to tell the Griffins."

After another second of contemplation, Hailey took a deep breath, and then said, "Okay."

"Okay?" Valerie studied Hailey to make sure she was certain, her excitement rising. "Tomorrow?"

"After the Christmas pageant," Hailey clarified. "When we're at home. And we need to tell them not to tell anyone else."

Valerie wished Hailey would let her tell

everyone—but, for now, she was happy that she'd at least let her tell Wade and his kids.

"I promise," Valerie assured her.

"Can you pray for me now?" Hailey asked.

"Of course."

Valerie said a prayer for Hailey, gave her a quick kiss on the forehead and then turned off the lights and left her room.

She went into her own bedroom and stood for a moment at the window overlooking the front lawn.

The snow was still falling and the soft light from the streetlamps glowed up and down the road. On the opposite corner was a large Victorian home owned by Max and Piper Evans. They used it as a bed-and-breakfast and lived in the third-floor apartment. But, with the addition of their second child on the way, Valerie wondered how much longer they would stay in the apartment. She knew them from church, but their daughter, Lainey, was too young to attend school.

For years, Valerie had looked at couples like Max and Piper, wondering when—or if—she'd ever find a love like theirs. Now, as she thought about the feelings stirring within her for Wade, she marveled at how blessed she felt. Yet a niggle of doubt plagued her. What would he say or do when he learned that Hailey was Valerie's daughter? Would he understand? See her side? Or would he be angry and disillusioned? Would he reject her and her love?

Even though she knew better, Valerie had started to fall in love with Wade. And it was nothing like how she had felt for Soren all those years ago in high school. That had been a surface-level attraction. Nothing more. And when something difficult had come their way, the relationship had crumbled under the weight of it.

What she felt for Wade was much different. She knew that hardships would come. She knew that difficulties, trials and tests were unavoidable. But she also knew that Wade was a man of integrity, sacrificial love and commitment. He had already stood up under the test of hardship and had come out the other side a stronger man. If something difficult came their way, he wouldn't run. He'd stay by her side and walk through it with her.

That was the kind of man she wanted to love—and, perhaps, marry.

As she got ready for bed, she prayed that he would understand why she hadn't told him the truth about Hailey. And that he would be willing to overcome the past with her, so they could have a future together.

Friday morning and afternoon felt like a blur to Wade as he finished his last day of school before the break. He had three class periods that day, and in between playing holiday games, like musical chairs with the "Rudolph the Red-Nosed Reindeer" song, they also ate treats and practiced a few of the songs they would be singing at the pageant that night.

Between classes, Wade was in the church sanctuary, working on last-minute changes to the set, lights and sound.

The only part of his day that didn't feel like a blur was seeing Valerie. When they were together, it felt like time stood still—for just a minute—and he loved it. Since she oversaw all the lunch periods, he didn't get to see her during his lunch break, but they did bump into each other getting coffee in the morning and afternoon. He knew exactly when she refilled her cup—and he was there every day to spend a few stolen moments with her.

As he drove home from school that afternoon with Issy and Brayden, his thoughts should have been on the program that evening. Instead, they were on Valerie and the sweet moment they had shared behind the church the night before. As well as the tender smiles she'd offered him today at school. There was an excitement in her gaze that made her eyes sparkle. He hoped it was because of him. As much as he was looking forward to the pageant tonight and showcasing the kids' talents to their parents—he was more excited about going to Valerie's house afterward and spending some time with her. Maybe they could light a fire in the den fireplace and have a few moments alone.

His thoughts were so distracted that as he pulled into his driveway, it almost didn't register that his mom's car was parked there.

"Grammy!" Brayden said when he saw it.

Wade frowned, not sure why his mom would be at his house when she knew they would be at the school until now.

The kids ran toward the house as Wade took his shoulder bag from the passenger seat.

"Grammy!" he heard his kids calling as they opened the front door.

Wade finally made it inside and closed the door to the chilly afternoon air. It had stopped snowing, but the forecast was threatening snow again. Wade just hoped it wouldn't interfere with the Christmas pageant that evening. After today, he didn't care about the weather—but it needed to hold off for a few more hours.

"Mom?" Wade asked as he hung his coat and bag on the coat-tree by the door.

"We're in here," his mom called, probably from the kitchen.

When Wade turned the corner, he found his mom standing at the island, chopping a carrot, and his dad was sitting on a stool.

Why were both his parents here?

"What's going on?" Wade asked, not surprised they had let themselves in. Ever since Wade had become a single dad, his parents had been there to help him. They had an extra key and were known to pop in from time to time or pick up the kids when there was an emergency and Wade couldn't get them in time. Other times, his mom would run over and do a couple loads of laundry, or vacuum, or clean something that needed attention. Wade had never complained. He knew she wasn't doing it to be critical of his own housekeeping skills, but to be helpful.

"We knew tonight was going to be busy for you," his mom said as she put the chopped carrots into a large stockpot on the stove. "I thought I'd make supper here and you won't have to worry about feeding the kids before you leave for the church."

"That was thoughtful," Wade said as he gave her a side hug. "Thank you."

"I came to ask you when you'll be coming back to work," his dad said as he picked up one of the peeled carrots and took a bite. "We have a remodeling job that came up and I need to have every man on hand to help."

"Is Mrs. Cole coming back after the first of the year?" his mom asked.

Wade took a seat next to his dad, needing to be off his feet while he spoke to his parents about this sensitive topic.

Especially because he had spent all

night thinking about Valerie's offer, and he wanted to pursue the option. See what it would look like to be a full-time music teacher. It wouldn't pay as much—but teachers received free education for their children, which was a big chunk of Wade's expenses. And, with some good budgeting, he could easily make ends meet.

"Mrs. Cole isn't planning to return at all," Wade told his parents.

"Is it that bad with her daughter and granddaughter?" his mom asked.

"No. The baby is doing well, but she won't be able to come home until February. Mrs. Cole wants to stay with her even after the baby is released from the hospital. She was going to retire this year anyway and decided to do it sooner than later."

"What does that mean about the teaching position?"

"It means that it's up for grabs. Valerie will be looking for a permanent replacement." He looked from his mom to his dad—knowing that his dad wouldn't take the next part easily. But he had to say it, not only to stand up for himself—but to stand up for his children, too. He didn't want to saddle them with Griffin Construction Company like his dad had tried to force it upon him. "She asked me if I'd be interested in the position."

"You told her no, right?" his dad asked.

"I told her I'd think about it."

"You can't be serious, Wade." His dad sat up straight on his stool. "You're taking over Griffin Construction one day. You've been working your whole life to run the company."

"No." Wade shook his head, digging deep to find the courage to speak to his father. "*You've* been working your whole life for me to run the company. You've never asked me what I want."

"You'd be foolish to turn down the offer to take on the family company," his dad continued. "Some people would give their right arm for this opportunity. It's a well-established business and it's given your mom and me a good life. Why would you want to throw away all our hard work for you to become a *music teacher*?"

"I'm sorry." Wade shook his head. "The company business was your dream, Dad, not mine. I would never assume that my dream is Issy's dream or Brayden's dream. I wouldn't start a business and then expect them to take it on, without wondering what they want to do with their life."

"I've worked hard to have a legacy to pass on to you." His dad's face had turned red as he listened to Wade's impassioned speech. "It wasn't about me—it was about you."

The guilt from his dad's words weighed heavily on Wade—but it wasn't justified guilt. "That was your choice. Not mine. I've wanted to work with music since I was a kid. I love teaching and I've enjoyed coordinating this upcoming Christmas pageant. It's something I could see myself doing for the rest of my life. It's fun to shape the minds and hearts of students. It's the legacy *I* want to pass down."

"This is your fault." His dad turned to

his mom. "If you hadn't encouraged him to take the temporary position, maybe he'd still be working for me."

"My fault?" His mom's face filled with indignation. "If it wasn't now, it would be later. Can't you see Wade's been unhappy all these years? You and I thought we were doing him a favor, but he's hated working for the family business. There's nothing we can do about that."

"Who will take it over?" his dad asked as he turned back to Wade.

"I don't know." Wade wanted to tell his dad it wasn't his problem to worry about, but he felt some sense of responsibility. After all, he'd been working for his dad for years under the understanding that someday Wade would take over the business. It wasn't what he wanted, but it was understood, nonetheless.

His dad stood. "I can see that my sacrifice has meant nothing to you. All these years, I worked for what? For my ungrateful son to throw it all back in my face."

"I'm not ungrateful—"

"You're the epitome of ungratefulness. You've made a mockery of my life's work."

"I've done no such thing." Wade was starting to get angry. "You have a lot to be proud of, Dad. You've provided well for Mom, and you've employed dozens of people who have been able to take care of their families. You've helped countless citizens with hundreds of home and business projects. You have nothing to be embarrassed or ashamed of. The best thing might be to sell the business when you and mom want to retire and live comfortably for the rest of your lives."

"That's easy for you to say." His dad shook his head. "You don't care."

"Fred." His mom sighed. "You know that's not true. And just like you, Wade needs to make his own choices. Your father didn't force you into a career or profession that you didn't want. Can you imagine if your dad had guilted you into taking over the sanitary pumping business? You would have been miserable driving a sewage truck all over town and doing the same work over and over again. Why would you assume Wade would want your business?"

His dad had nothing to say to her logic, so he simply scowled.

His mom turned to Wade. "If this is what you want, then go after it. You only live once. God has given you the talent and the ability to make and teach music. And He's provided an opportunity for you to pursue your passion, while providing a good education for your kids, a comfortable home to live in and a sound income. I know you'll need to make some adjustments, but just think, you could still work for Griffin Construction during the summer months when school is on break, if you like."

"I would like that," Wade said as he focused on his dad, "if you'll let me."

His dad shook his head and waved a hand at Wade, as if to tell him to move along.

"I don't need it," Wade began, "but I

would like your blessing, Dad. I've made up my mind and I'm planning to pursue this opportunity, but that doesn't mean that your opinion doesn't matter."

His dad harrumphed, but his mom said, "You have our blessing, Wade. Maybe not Dad's at the moment, but he'll come around. I've known him for four decades and it takes him some time to accept change. But he does. And he will."

"Thanks." Wade smiled at his mom.

"Now," she said. "Let's get this soup made and then I will help Issy and Brayden get ready for their performance tonight."

Wade couldn't wait to tell Valerie what he had decided. He would have a lot of work in the near future to get all the licensing he needed, but it would be worth the trouble.

He was about to start a new chapter in his life and he hoped and prayed Valerie would be at the center of it all.

Chapter Thirteen

Valerie didn't know if she was coming or going on Friday. The last day of the semester was always busy, but with the Christmas break about to start, and the pageant just hours away, the students were anxious and restless. There had been two disciplinary events she needed to manage on top of all her other responsibilities.

But no matter how busy she was, she still took time to talk to Wade when she saw him in the teachers' lounge. He was a bright and calming part of her day, and even though they only had a moment together, that moment had sustained her through the rest of her work.

If she didn't have Hailey, she would have stayed at the school after the final bell and worked until the families began to arrive for the evening program—but she did have Hailey and she didn't want her daughter to feel like she lived at the school. They splurged for supper and went out to eat at a local pizza place and then went home to change into their Christmas pageant clothing. Valerie helped Hailey with her stage makeup and then they returned to the school before anyone else.

Now, as Valerie greeted families as they entered the church for the evening program, she started to let herself think about what would happen *after* the Christmas pageant, when Wade and his kids came over to her house. She had spoken to him briefly when he arrived at the church, but there was so much to do, they hadn't discussed anything important.

That would come later.

The church was beginning to fill as people came in out of the snow. Parents, siblings, aunts, uncles, grandparents and family friends were entering the building. Valerie stood by the sanctuary doors, welcoming people as students stood nearby, handing out programs. A large Christmas tree sat in the corner of the foyer and pine garlands hung over the doors. The festive lights added an ambiance to the building that gave Valerie all the holiday feelings she loved.

"Welcome," Valerie said to the Ashers, a prominent family who lived in a beautiful historic mansion on the banks of the Mississippi River. Several of their children, including Ryan, the student playing Joseph, attended the school. "Merry Christmas."

"Merry Christmas," they said as they took a program. They visited with Valerie for a few moments and then entered the sanctuary.

Valerie said hello to Knox and Merritt Taylor, whose twin girls attended and were playing angels tonight. She also greeted the pastor, Jake Dawson, and his lovely wife, Kate. Their oldest daughter, Maggie, was a student and would be one of the narrators. Jake and Kate's triplets, all boys, came in with them, while Kate held their small daughter on her hip.

"We can't wait for tonight's performance," Kate said to Valerie. "Everyone is so pleased with Wade's job. And the kids seem to really like him. We're thankful he stepped up to help."

"So am I," Valerie said with a smile. Kate had been a Broadway actress before she had come to Timber Falls and sang on the worship team. To know that she was happy with Wade's job meant a lot.

As they moved past, the front door opened again, and a familiar woman entered with the swirling snow.

"Mom?" Valerie whispered to herself, her heart rate escalating.

Her mom looked around the entry hall with a slight frown, searching each face until her gaze rested on Valerie.

A smile lit up her eyes and she started to move toward Valerie.

Valerie left her spot near the sanctuary doors and met her mom in the middle of the entry hall. Dozens of people mingled around her, some just entering the building, while others were taking off their coats and hanging them in the back hall.

"Mom!" Valerie said, almost speechless. "What are you doing here?"

"I started to feel so guilty about how I left Hailey. The last time I spoke to her, my heart was breaking. I thought it would be fun to surprise her and see her playing Mary tonight."

"Where is your husband?"

"He stayed in Arizona. I wasn't sure I wanted him to come. Not because I'm embarrassed or anything," she said quickly, "but because I thought it would be good to just be the three of us. You know? You, me and Hailey. There are things we need to discuss, and I thought he'd feel out of place."

"Discuss?" Valerie asked, still trying to grapple with the fact that her mom had come. Why did she insist on surprising and shocking Valerie? Couldn't she call first?

"I shouldn't have left the way I did," her mom continued. "Looking back, I see it was thoughtless of me. But I didn't want you to try to talk me out of marrying Lyle."

Several people passed Valerie, smiling their hellos. Valerie didn't want her mom to say something she should not in front of these people. And the discussion they needed to have would have to wait until later.

Except...

"I have guests coming to the house after the program," Valerie said, her heart starting to fall. She couldn't ask Wade to come over now—not like this.

"We don't have to talk tonight," her mom said. "I'm planning to stay until Christmas

Day. We'll have plenty of time. I can wait at the hotel and come tomorrow."

"You don't need to stay at a hotel." Valerie was trying to gather her thoughts and make a plan of action. "I have a spare room. You should stay with us."

"Are you sure?"

"I can't ask my mom to stay in a hotel when I have room." Valerie took a deep breath. She'd figure this out. She had to.

"If you're sure."

"I am." Valerie nodded, scrambling to think of a way to make everything work. She wanted Wade to meet her mom, but she needed to explain things to him beforehand. "Perhaps you can take Hailey back to my house after the program. I will need to stay behind to close the building." It wasn't quite true since Wade had a key and could close up without her. But she needed some time alone with him to tell him about Hailey. "If you take her to my house, it will give you two time to talk." She'd find a way to tell Wade then. It wouldn't be perfect, but it would be necessary. Then he and the kids could come over and meet her mom.

"That will work." Her mom smiled. She was an older version of Valerie and if anyone saw them together, they'd know they were related. There would be questions—questions Valerie wanted to answer on her own. In her own way.

With a quick glance at the clock, Valerie realized the program was about to start. And she needed to get to the front of the sanctuary to officially welcome everyone.

Valerie walked her mom into the sanctuary and led her to the front where a spot had been saved for the principal. No doubt Hailey would see her mom from the stage and be very surprised. Hopefully it wouldn't cause her to mess up her lines or her performance—but it couldn't be helped.

"Have a seat," Valerie said to her mom and then went to the stage at the front of the room. Her hands were still shaking from her mom's unexpected arrival, but she took a deep breath and forced herself to become the professional, disciplined principal they had all hired. She had met most of them, but for the others, this was their first glimpse of the new administrator. And she wanted to make a good impression.

"Welcome to the Timber Falls Christian School's annual Christmas pageant," she said as the room quieted. "The children have been working for weeks to bring you this performance tonight. They are excited and eager to share this beautiful story with you. The story of the Christ Child's arrival into our world. May this evening remind you of the miracle of His birth and the joy of His presence in all our lives." The audience applauded and Valerie glanced to the side of the stage where Wade had appeared.

He smiled at her, and she smiled back, her heart beating hard for a new reason.

She hoped he would understand why she had kept the truth from him for so long.

"I would be remiss not to introduce all of you to the man responsible for tonight's performance," Valerie continued. "Mr. Wade Griffin graciously stepped into the long-term subbing position when Mrs. Cole was called away. As all of you know from your students, the children have loved having him as their music teacher. And, as all the staff, board members and volunteers at the school know, we love having him on our team. Tonight, each of you will see his love for music and his joy in sharing it with the students. Mr. Griffin?" Valerie waved him over.

He came to the middle of the stage with her, and she couldn't help but feel a rush of pleasure at the applause he received. He was wearing a pair of slacks, a button-down shirt and a Christmas tie. He looked calm, confident and happy to be there. And when his gaze connected with Valerie's, she was certain the entire room would see her feelings for him written all over her face. She couldn't help it. She'd fallen in love with Wade, and it was hard to hide.

"Thank you," Wade said to her and then to the room, "I am thrilled at the progress I've seen in your students. I hope you enjoy tonight's performance."

After another round of applause, Valerie and Wade left the stage and he came to the pew to sit with her.

He paused when he saw her mom and she quickly whispered, "My mom surprised us with a visit. I'll introduce you afterward."

Wade nodded, but he smiled at Valerie's mom before he took a seat.

Valerie sat between them as the lights dimmed.

She felt Wade's gaze on her and turned to him. He had a look of concern on his face. No doubt he had a lot of questions. All he knew about her mom was that she had abandoned Hailey. Valerie tried to smile, to reassure him that everything was okay. Even though she wasn't sure it was.

The pew was tight, especially with her mom's unexpected presence—but Valerie didn't mind sitting so close to Wade. Their shoulders pressed together and neither one shifted to move.

The show began with the narrators coming on stage. As they shared the beginning of the Christmas story, Hailey and Ryan appeared at the back of the sanctuary and made their way down the aisle toward the stage.

Hailey was dressed in a long blue robe with a white shawl over her head. Ryan was dressed in a similar fashion, but he had a staff in one hand while he kept his other arm around Hailey's back.

When they arrived at the stage, an innkeeper told them there was no room for them, so they found a stable and when the spotlight shifted back to the narrators, Valerie watched Hailey put a doll into the manger. Then she looked up and her gaze landed on Valerie in the front row—and quickly slipped to her mom.

Hailey's eyes widened, and she looked like she was going to rise and come off the stage, but she must have thought better of it and stayed in place. Since the spotlight was on the narrators, no one would be watching Hailey.

Her mom gave her a little wave and the look of excitement on Hailey's face was bittersweet. Valerie was happy that Hailey was pleased to see her mom—but, at the same time, she was sad that Hailey never seemed that happy to see her. If given the choice, would Hailey still go back with her mom? Wasn't the life she had to offer Hailey one that she wanted?

Valerie pushed all those thoughts aside and watched as the pageant continued. There were a few slipups here and there, but it was a beautiful performance—and they had Wade to thank for all of it.

When the spotlight was back on the manger, and the wise men arrived to bring gifts to the Christ Child, Ryan stood up, his face fierce as he said, "Who goes there?"

It wasn't part of the script—and Wade grew tense beside Valerie.

The first wise man frowned and looked at Ryan, then said, "It's me—the first wise man."

Ryan eased a bit and said, "I was just checking. It's my job to protect Mary and Jesus."

The crowd chuckled—and then the show went on as planned.

Valerie glanced up at Wade and he smiled down at her before taking her hand into his and giving it a gentle squeeze.

Her heart filled with an intense love and adoration for the man beside her—and she didn't care who knew.

Wade tried to focus on the Christmas pageant. After all, he'd spent weeks of hard work for this one night. But all he could think about was Valerie's hand in his. He shouldn't have taken it—what would people think? Yet—he couldn't help it. He wanted to touch her, to be as close to her as possible. His feelings for her were so strong and intense, he couldn't stop them from spilling over into his words and actions and behaviors.

He couldn't wait for this evening to tell her that he wanted to proceed with licensing and become the permanent music teacher. It might be strange to have Valerie as his boss, but as far as he knew, there were no rules against it, and he loved knowing that his job was secure in her capable hands. He wasn't intimidated by her authority or troubled by the idea that she had the power to hire and fire him. He trusted her. Completely.

More than that, he was looking forward to this evening because it felt like a new beginning. With her mom's arrival, he hoped Valerie would finally trust him with her past. He wanted her to feel safe enough to share her pain and heartache. He wanted her to know that he was there for her, to carry the burden of whatever had happened in her life—and whatever was to come.

He hoped she was feeling the same way about him—and the fact that she let him hold her hand was a good sign that she did have the same feelings. He wanted to tell her what was in his heart and find a way forward. The hard part was done—finding a woman he could trust again. Life wouldn't always be easy but loving her would be and he hoped she'd give him the chance.

The nativity play ended, and all the kids lined up around the room to sing the final song of the night. Wade let go of Valerie's hand and the two of them walked to the center of the stage. The lights were turned off and the kids began to flip on their battery-operated candles. As the pianist began to play "Silent Night," Wade and Valerie joined the children to sing the sweet, melodic song. The children's faces were sweet, and the candles made their eyes shine.

Several people wiped tears from their cheeks as the children sang, and when it was done, the room erupted in applause.

"Thank you all for coming," Valerie said to the audience. "Merry Christmas!"

The children left their places and found their loved ones in the room. It was loud and chaotic, but parents and grandparents were eager to congratulate their little stars. Issy and Brayden came to Wade as Valerie left his side and joined Hailey and her mom.

Hailey ran up to Valerie's mom and threw herself into her arms.

Her mom lifted her off the ground and held her tight, closing her eyes.

The look on Valerie's face was not happiness or excitement—it was a troubled look, filled with a depth of sadness that broke his heart. Had Valerie's mom come to take Hailey back? Was that why Valerie looked so upset?

A pang of sadness filled Wade's heart for Issy. What would his daughter think if Hailey left Timber Falls? In Wade's mind, Valerie and Hailey belonged together. As he pictured a possible future with Valerie, he had assumed that Hailey was part of the package. He hated to think of the gaping hole in all their lives if Hailey left.

"Who is that with Hailey?" Issy asked, following Wade's gaze.

"I think that's her mom," Wade said.

Issy left Wade's side before he could stop her and approached Hailey as her mom was setting her down.

Wade followed, not wanting Issy to intrude on this moment.

"Is this your mom?" Issy asked Hailey.

Hailey glanced between her mom and Valerie, a strange look on her face. She shook her head. "This is my grandma. Valerie is my mom."

Wade stopped in his tracks as Valerie turned her ashen face toward him.

And, in a heartbeat, he saw the truth.

Valerie was Hailey's mom—and she'd lied to him.

"Miss Wilmington is your mom?" Issy asked with wide, confused eyes.

"She was young when I was born, so she gave me to her mom," Hailey said matter-of-factly. "I only saw Valerie at Christmastime, until a couple months ago when I moved in with her."

"Hailey," Valerie said in a strained voice. "We can talk about this later."

Valerie's mom looked uncomfortable as her gaze swiveled between Valerie and Wade—and then back to Valerie. "You didn't tell anyone the truth? You led them to believe that Hailey was your sister?"

People were passing by them, some looking like they wanted to stop and talk to Valerie and Wade—but they all continued. It was clear there was tension among their little group.

Tension that was coiling so tight inside Wade, he felt like he had been punched. Why had Valerie misled him? Especially when he had told her how much he valued truth? No wonder she avoided telling him about her past whenever he brought it up. He was sick to his stomach at all the lies—all the times she had misled him.

"Hailey wasn't ready for people to know," Valerie said in a choked voice. "I wanted—"

"Hailey wasn't ready, or you weren't?" her mom asked, clearly disappointed in her daughter.

"I—" Valerie swallowed hard, then turned to Wade, her eyes filled with uncertainty and fear. "I'm sorry."

He couldn't even respond. She'd opened a dormant wound that Amber had inflicted with her web of lies and mistruths, leaving his heart feeling raw and battered again. He had trusted Valerie—was about to declare his love for her—yet he didn't know her. If she couldn't share one of the most important details of her life with Wade—the fact that she was a mother—then what else might she be hiding?

"Issy," Wade said, "get your coat. We need to leave."

Valerie stepped forward. "Please—can we go somewhere and talk?"

His back was rigid as he addressed her. "I don't have anything to say to you, Valerie. And, frankly, whatever you say to me from here on out, I'll struggle to believe. I think it's best that I leave."

"But—won't you come over?" Her voice was desperate—just like Amber's had been when she was caught in her lies, and she was trying to manipulate him. "I want to explain."

He shook his head, but his anger was quickly becoming replaced with a sadness so deep and aching, he struggled to breathe. "There's nothing you can say that can make this better." He started to walk away, but turned back and said, "And consider this my resignation. I couldn't work for someone I don't trust."

"Daddy," Issy said as she tried to keep

up with him. "I thought we were going to Hailey's house tonight."

"Not anymore, Bug." He tried to control his voice, but his emotions were getting the best of him. He had to take a second to pull them together before he said, "We need to get home. It's been a long day."

He tried to smile at those he passed, but he had to get out of there before he made a fool of himself.

"Daddy," Issy said as they put on their coats, "what's wrong? Why are you mad at Miss Wilmington?"

He swallowed the emotions clogging his throat and prayed Valerie wouldn't come after him. He couldn't face her—not here, not in front of all these people. He just wanted to get home. To put his kids to bed, and then—he wasn't sure. He should have known this was going to happen. He had tried to prevent himself from giving his heart to someone who would do this very thing. Hadn't he learned his lesson from Amber? It was better to not trust anyone—that way, they couldn't hurt him this deeply.

But it wasn't just the pain of being lied to—it was the pain of losing something—someone—he had started to dream about. He had loved Valerie, wanted to spend every day with her. Now, it was all gone. In one, simple moment.

"I'm mad because she's not the person I thought she was," he said as he opened the back door and led his kids out to his truck.

"Wade!"

His kids were in the truck, and he was about to get in when he heard his name.

It was his mom.

"Where are you running off to?" she asked, wrapping her arms around herself since she hadn't taken the time to grab her coat.

"I need to get home."

"You didn't give Dad and I enough time to find you in the sanctuary. I didn't get to take any pictures with the kids. What's going on?"

He took a deep breath, realizing how rash he'd been. He should have stayed to help Valerie put things away and close the church for the night. Granted, there were dozens of volunteers who would help—but he should have been part of the team to oversee it. But he couldn't face her. He was afraid of what he might say and do—revealing the depth of his pain in front of everyone. Valerie would see that it was taken care of—she would have stayed anyway.

"Tell Dad I'm not taking the job here at the school. I'll be back to work for the family company the day after Christmas." Even as he said the words, his heart clenched. This was yet another loss on the pile that was stacking up before him. Another dream that he would have to mourn.

His mom approached and put her hand on Wade's arm. "What's going on, son?"

He let out a sigh and shook his head. He trusted his mom—even if she could be controlling at times, she was a great confidante. "Valerie isn't Hailey's sister—she's her mom."

"Valerie is Hailey's *mom*?" Her eyes went wide.

"But she decided to lie to me—and to all of us—and not tell us the truth."

"Did she say why she lied?"

"Something about Hailey not being ready to tell people—but I know that's a cop-out. She had ample opportunity to tell me the truth and she decided to let me believe the lie instead. I can't work for a woman I don't trust."

"You're in love with her." His mom's mouth parted. "You are, aren't you?"

"What does it matter?" He wasn't going to deny it. "She's no better than Amber."

His mom took a step back, shock on her face. "How could you even compare them? Amber was manipulative, secretive, selfish and controlling. She lied to you for years to cover up her transgressions. She deliberately hurt you, and continued hurting you even once you knew the truth. Valerie has done nothing like that. The secret she kept from you was from an event that happened in her life ten years ago. Hailey was thrust upon her without warning a couple months ago, and she was grappling with the truth. I'm sure Hailey was, too—and she didn't want people to know something about her that made her feel ashamed or different than the other children. You can't blame her. Valerie was in a tough place, Wade. I think you should hear her out. She doesn't seem manipulative or selfish."

He took several deep breaths, knowing his mother spoke truth—yet he was not able to face Valerie. His pain was too fresh—too deep.

"Valerie isn't Amber." His mom studied him closely. "What you're feeling right now is the pain Amber inflicted on you. Her motives and reasons were not the same as Valerie's. You can't punish Valerie for something Amber did in the past. Please—don't throw this new relationship away. Valerie is a wonderful woman and she's perfect for you."

He stared at the back door of the church—half hoping Valerie would appear and half hoping he could get away to think and be alone.

"I need to leave," he said to his mom. "I need some time and space."

His mom nodded. "I'll hold off on telling your dad that you're coming back to the construction company. Take some time to think. Don't make rash decisions in the middle of your pain."

"Good night, Mom." Wade gave her a hug and then got into his truck.

The kids were quiet in the backseat as he pulled out of the parking lot. No doubt they sensed Wade's mood.

But when they passed by a streetlamp, and Wade glanced into the rearview mirror, he saw tears on Issy's face.

"What's wrong, Bug?" he asked his daughter.

"I want to go to Hailey's house," she said

as she wiped her cheek. "And I want you to marry Miss Wilmington."

Wade let out a breath. "I'm sorry. Neither of those things is possible."

It was all he could say.

Chapter Fourteen

Valerie hadn't slept most of the night. She had stayed at the church to oversee the cleanup and had gone to her office to have some time alone after everyone left. Her heart was breaking, and she had no one to blame but herself. Every time she closed her eyes, all she could see was the look on Wade's face when Hailey had told Issy the truth. She wasn't angry that he had left early—she didn't blame him. But she was sad—sadder than she'd been since leaving Hailey behind and moving to college.

Her mom had taken Hailey home right after the show, and when Valerie had finally come home, well after eleven, both were already in bed sleeping.

Now, as she stood in her kitchen the next morning, staring out her back window with a cup of coffee in hand, she was exhausted, heartsore and miserable. She'd fallen in love with Wade Griffin, and she was afraid it was too late. All the hopes and dreams she'd started to tend in her heart were shriveling up and dying right before her eyes—and there was nothing she could do to stop them.

"Want to talk?" Her mom entered the kitchen in her pajamas, her blond hair in a ponytail.

"I don't think there's anything I can say." Valerie hadn't confided in her mom since high school. It had been so long since they'd spent considerable time together. In some ways, her mom felt like a stranger. Yet—she probably knew Valerie better than anyone else.

"There's always something to be said." Her mom found a mug and filled it with coffee. "I hope you don't mind that I made myself at home last night."

"Of course not." Valerie turned away from the window and faced her mom. Her eyes were gritty from lack of sleep and crying most of the night. She hadn't even had the courage to look at herself in the mirror when she was brushing her teeth. She probably looked like a swollen, red mess.

"Come on," her mom said. "Let's go sit by the Christmas tree."

Valerie followed her mom into the living room. Annabelle had come down to eat breakfast and go out but had found her way into the living room and was sleeping on one of the couches. Hailey hadn't come down yet, and Valerie was going to let her sleep in. That was what holiday vacations were for.

They each took a seat on one of the couches closest to the Christmas tree, facing each other. Valerie had plugged in the tree when she came down, and with the overcast sky outside, it offered a warm, welcoming light in the room.

Steam swirled up from her mom's cup as she took a sip and closed her eyes with a sigh. When she opened them, she offered Valerie a sad smile. "I know I haven't been much of a mom to you these past ten years, but I'm here to talk, Val. Even if I don't have good advice, I can listen."

Valerie hadn't poured her heart out in years. She'd kept the secret about Hailey for so long, it seemed strange to speak openly about it—even with her mom, who knew the truth.

"Is this about that music teacher?" her mom asked. "I saw him take your hand last night. I could instantly see how much you two care for each other."

Tears burned Valerie's eyes as she looked down at her mug. "I didn't tell him the truth about Hailey and now he won't be able to trust me again." She told her mom about Wade's ex-wife and how hard it was for him to trust her.

"Did you really keep the truth from everyone because Hailey asked you to?" her mom asked.

"Yes. It's the only reason. I knew it would be hard to tell people the truth—but I was ready. Each time I brought it up to her, she begged me not to tell. She said that you are her mom and that's how she wanted to keep things."

"I'm sorry I made a false assumption last night. I'm the one who put you in this tight position and I'm sorry." Her mom sighed. "For what it's worth, I think you need to try to talk to him again."

"I want to, but I don't know if he'll believe me."

"He might need some time. In a few days, reach out to him and see if he'll let you explain."

Valerie nodded. "If he'll let me."

They both took a sip of their coffee and then her mom let out a deep breath. "I wasn't quite honest with you when I told you I came because I missed Hailey." She set her coffee cup down. "I mean, I do miss Hailey—more than I thought possible. But I came because I realized I made a mistake. I shouldn't have left her here with you."

"Do you regret marrying Lyle?"

"No. But I should have told him from the beginning that Hailey and I went together. If he wanted me, he got her, too. He could have sold his house in the retirement community, and we could have purchased something somewhere else— actually, that's what I got him to agree to. I told him I was coming back to get Hailey."

Valerie's heart dropped for the second time in twenty-four hours, and she stared at her mom. "What?"

"I know you don't want her, so I—"

"What do you mean, I don't want her? I do want Hailey. I love her. I've never felt so whole or complete before in my life. I can't imagine being without her now."

Her mom frowned. "Truly?"

Valerie nodded. "Dropping her off with

me was the best thing you could have done. We've started to build a life that I love—and I hope she loves it, too."

Her mom was quiet for a moment and then said, "I told Hailey last night that she could move to Arizona with me. I didn't think you'd mind."

"Mind?" Valerie stood, her anger rising. "How could you do something like that without talking to me? First, you bring her here without talking to me—and then you plan to take her away without asking me what I want? Hailey needs stability in her life. We were just starting to get into a good routine. She has wonderful friends, she's getting excellent grades and she is looking forward to the plans we've made—and so am I."

"I took Hailey from you ten years ago when you weren't in a position to raise her—"

"But I am now."

"I put in all the hard work—you didn't."

"You're right—I didn't. But I want to now."

Her mom set down her mug on the coffee table and stood to face Valerie. "I would win a custody battle, if it came to that."

Valerie's mouth slipped open as she stared at her mom. "You'd do that to me?"

"I miss her, Valerie. You don't know what it's like to raise a child and then suddenly not see her for months on end."

"No—I don't. But I know what it's like to give birth to one and then not be part of her life for ten years. And I don't want to miss another moment."

"I think the person we need to ask is Hailey."

Valerie took a deep breath. "I know what she'll choose."

"If it's what I want—and what she wants—then you'll need to let her go, Valerie."

Shaking her head, Valerie said, "I don't want to." Her heart was already shattered by the look on Wade's face when he learned she'd lied to him. She couldn't bear saying goodbye to Hailey, too. She'd be all alone—exactly as she'd been two months ago. Yet now she knew what she was missing. Her life would feel void and empty. The thought filled her with such despair, she could hardly breathe.

"What if she chooses to stay?" Valerie asked, trying not to feel desperate or panicky. "Will you let her go without a fight?"

"If she wants to stay, then I will honor her wishes. I don't want to traumatize her more than I have already—but if she wants to come with me, I'll insist you let her."

It was the hardest thing Valerie had ever done, but she nodded. "I won't fight both of you, either."

"Should we wake her up and ask her?" her mom asked.

"No. Let's let her wake up and have some breakfast before we bombard her with such a difficult decision." Valerie wanted to ask if Hailey had given her mom any indication the night before what she wanted, but she couldn't bring herself to ask. Instead, she left the living room and began to make breakfast.

Cooking relaxed her like nothing else— yet, this time, it didn't ease her anxiety.

About twenty minutes later, Hailey came downstairs, bleary-eyed and sleepy.

Valerie entered the living room as Hailey stopped at the bottom of the stairs. When she saw her mom, her face brightened and she said, "I wasn't dreaming! You're still here."

"Of course I'm still here." Her mother held out her arms and Hailey ran to her, climbing onto her lap to snuggle.

Valerie felt a twinge of jealousy and her heart began to hurt, knowing what Hailey would choose.

"Are you hungry?" Valerie asked. "I made your favorite pancakes."

Hailey nodded and jumped off her mom's lap to run to the kitchen.

When they all had filled their plates, they took them to the dining room to begin breakfast. But Valerie had no appetite and she absently cut her pancakes, unable to eat them.

"You did such a wonderful job as Mary in the pageant," her mom said to Hailey. "Did it take a lot to memorize your part?"

"No." Hailey shook her head. "It was easy."

"Do you think you'd like to do more plays in the future?"

"Maybe." Hailey shrugged as she shoved a forkful into her mouth. "Issy said her dad wants to plan a spring musical for the school. I'd kind of like to be in it."

Valerie had heard Wade talk about a spring musical and had loved the idea. But now she wasn't sure if it would even happen—or if Hailey would be here to participate.

"If you come to Arizona with me," her mom said carefully, "then you couldn't be in the spring musical."

Hailey frowned and looked at Valerie.

"Mom told me," Valerie said, trying not

to sound upset. "I want you to know that you are more than welcome to stay here, Hailey. I don't want you to go to Arizona. I want you to stay here with me. But, if you want to go—then I won't stop you. You have a right to choose."

Hailey looked at her mom next, a question in her eyes.

"And, like I said last night," her mom told her, "I would love for you to come to Arizona. It won't be the same as living in Saint Paul. Lyle will be there, and you'll go to a new school and meet new friends. But we'll have each other and that's all that matters."

"Will you be mad at me if I want to stay—with my mom?" Hailey asked.

Her mom shook her head. "No. I won't be mad. But whatever choice you make, it will be a permanent one. You can't go back and forth whenever you get mad at one of us."

"I'm sorry that you have to make this hard decision," Valerie said to Hailey. "I know it's not an easy one, but Mom and I don't want to make the choice for you. We both love you—and will continue loving you, no matter where you live. Neither one of us will be angry at you." She wanted to beg Hailey to stay, but she wouldn't do that to the child. It wasn't fair.

Annabelle sat on the floor next to Hailey, her tail wagging as she waited for a scrap from her plate. Hailey looked down at her and then back at her mom.

"I want to stay here."

Valerie's eyes filled with tears of relief and joy. She clasped her hands and laid them in her lap, trying not to jump up from the table to grab her daughter in her arms.

"Are you sure?" her mom asked Hailey.

"Yes. I love it here." She turned to Valerie. "Can I call you Mom?" She looked at Valerie's mom next. "And can I call you Grandma?"

The tears escaped Valerie's eyes as she nodded. "Yes—you can call me Mom."

Her mother was also crying—but for

a different reason, Valerie was sure. "Of course you can call me Grandma," her mom said. "And I'm happy you chose to stay with your mom, Hailey. I think it's the best choice. I will miss you, but I'll come to visit, and you can call me whenever you'd like."

Hailey grinned and nodded, then took another big bite of her pancake.

Valerie set down her napkin and excused herself. She went into the kitchen and leaned against the counter, letting the tears fall.

"Are you crying because you're happy again?" Hailey asked from the doorway.

Valerie opened her arms, and her daughter ran into her embrace. "Yes," she whispered. "I'm very happy."

Yet—she wasn't completely happy and wasn't sure she'd ever be again.

She missed Wade. Would he let her explain herself? She couldn't imagine how difficult it would be to wait a few days before contacting him, but if that's what it took, she'd wait forever.

Nothing had been going smoothly the past couple of days. Wade was irritable with his children, crabby with a cashier and annoyed with the traffic, which was ridiculous since Timber Falls' traffic was hardly enough to speak about. He wasn't sleeping well, and his exhaustion added to his bad mood.

It hadn't taken him long to realize that he was more upset with himself than with Valerie. His mom's talk out in the parking lot had resonated with him, yet he knew he needed some time to separate his feelings. It wasn't just about letting his emotions cool down after learning about Valerie's secret—it was more about coming to peace with the pain from his past with Amber. *If* Valerie allowed him to speak to her again—which he doubted after the way he'd treated her—he couldn't bring his wounds with him into a new relationship. It wasn't fair to him or to Valerie.

By Christmas Eve, three days after the pageant, he was crabbier than ever. He missed Valerie and he was getting tired of telling Issy that she couldn't invite Hailey over. His daughter obviously missed her friend, too.

"Anyone home?" Wade's dad asked as he walked into the house that afternoon.

"We're here," Wade called from the kitchen where he was putting lasagna into the oven for their Christmas Eve dinner. "Come in."

His dad entered with a baking pan in hand. "Your mom sent me over to give you this."

"What is it?"

"She said the kids needed cinnamon rolls for their Christmas breakfast tomorrow." His dad handed the pan over to Wade. "She just baked them fresh. They're still warm."

Wade took the cinnamon rolls and set

the pan on the counter, the scent of cinnamon wafting up. "Thanks."

His dad crossed his arms, still wearing his coat and boots, which told Wade he didn't plan to stay long. "Your mom said I need to talk some sense into you, too."

Wade let out a sigh, thankful his kids were playing in their rooms and wouldn't be privy to his dad's criticism. Wade was already feeling crabby and out of sorts. His dad might as well add to the irritation.

"Lay it on me. Tell me how disappointed you are in me. But did Mom tell you that I'm coming back to work for you?"

His dad frowned. "Now, that's the kind of nonsense you need to quit, right this minute."

It was Wade's turn to frown. "I thought you wanted me to come back to work for you."

"I do—believe me. But it's not what I want that matters. You were right. I made the choice to start a construction company and I didn't consult with you. I can't expect you to follow in my footsteps no more than my dad could expect me to do the same. So, get that out of your head. If you want to be a music teacher, be a music teacher. Don't let someone like me tell you otherwise."

Wade continued to frown. "It doesn't matter anyway. I resigned."

"When you got upset at Miss Wilmington?"

"Yes." Wade had immediately regretted the way he'd handled himself that night—but Valerie hadn't reached out to him, and he wasn't sure she'd want him to reach out to her.

"That's what your mom wanted me to talk to you about. I know I don't always say the right thing, or act the right way, but when I see something that's wrong, I say so. And letting that young lady go is wrong. If she likes you—and especially if she loves you—you should be on her doorstep this instant asking her for forgiveness."

"She lied to me."

"She withheld the truth—for reasons you haven't given her the chance to explain. Your mom told me all about it. The most important thing in a relationship is communication. If you can't talk and listen, then you'll never be happy."

"I used to talk to Amber all the time and all she did was lie to cover up other lies."

"Miss Wilmington isn't Amber, son. You know that. And, in your heart of hearts, you knew Amber was lying, didn't you? You can tell. When you talk to Valerie, listen to your gut. If you sense she's still lying, then walk away. But, if you know she's telling the truth, and she's open and vulnerable with you, then pursue her with abandon. No one is perfect, you know that. She made a mistake. We all do. Forgive her. That's what forgiveness is for."

Wade sat on one of the stools and put his face in his hands. "I want to."

"Then do it."

He looked up at his dad. "What if she doesn't want to talk to me?"

"Then, you have your answer. But right now, living in the what-ifs isn't helpful. Call her up. Invite her over. Open your heart. I know it takes courage—but love is worth the risk. Every single time."

Wade knew his dad was right—and was surprised he was being so eloquent and vulnerable. When his dad talked like this, Wade listened.

Wade also knew he was miserable without Valerie and wanted her in his life. If he spoke to her, and he sensed she wasn't being honest, he would have to find a way forward without her. But, if she was open and honest, like he knew she would be, he would have to overcome his own shortcomings and fears to offer his heart to her.

The only way he would know is if he put himself out there and took the risk.

"I should scoot," his dad said. "I still need to run to the grocery store for your mom. She's cooking up a storm. We'll see you tomorrow afternoon for Christmas dinner?"

"We'll be there."

"Good. There are so many presents under the tree, they've started to take over the living room. The kids will be opening them for hours." He waved. "We'll see you tomorrow."

"Thanks, Dad." Wade walked him to the front door. "I appreciate that you stopped by."

His dad did something uncharacteristic and gave Wade a hug. "I love you, son."

"I love you, too, Dad."

"Merry Christmas."

"Merry Christmas." Wade smiled as his dad left the house.

If Wade lived to be a hundred, his dad's actions today would still surprise him. He wasn't a touchy-feely person. He didn't open up often and Wade could count the times on his two hands that his dad said *I love you*. It was a Christmas gift in many ways and Wade would hold the memory close.

He closed the door and walked back into the kitchen, contemplating all the things his dad had said. Would Valerie still want to come over for Christmas Eve dinner? Or would it be best to wait until after Christmas to talk to her?

"Daddy?" Issy asked as she walked down the hallway from her bedroom, a friendship bracelet in hand. "Can I call Hailey? I made this bracelet for her, and I want to give it to her." Issy's brown eyes were large as she watched him. "Can I go over and see her?"

"I don't know—I haven't spoken to Valerie since the night of the pageant. I'm not sure if she'll want to talk to me, either."

"Call her," Issy said, taking Wade's hand and pulling him toward the cell-phone-charging station in the living room. "Tell her you're sorry and ask her to bring Hailey over. Or ask if we can go there."

"I don't know, Bug."

"Please. It's Christmas."

Wade wouldn't find more courage than he had in this moment. He sighed and Issy cheered, knowing she had convinced him.

He let her hand go and went to his cell phone. He picked it up, his gut turning with nerves, and found Valerie's number.

He stared at it for a heartbeat and then pressed the green call icon.

The phone rang once, twice—and by the third time, he was convinced she was going to ignore him.

"Hello?" she asked, her voice tentative.

"Valerie?" He walked away from Issy, who was staring at him with an intent gaze, and went to the dining room where the large picture window looked out at the Mississippi River. The water didn't freeze right behind his house and the waterfowl were playing there. Ducks, geese and a handful of trumpeter swans.

"Hi, Wade. I was just thinking about calling you."

His heart beat so hard, he was afraid

it might burst. Suddenly, he didn't know what to say or how to begin, so he said the first thing that came to mind. "Issy's been missing Hailey. She hasn't stopped asking me to call and see if they can get together."

"Oh." The one word sounded sad—disappointed. "Hailey's been bugging me, too."

He paced away from the window and shoved his free hand into his pocket. "I was wondering—if you want to, we have plenty of food—would you still like to come over for Christmas Eve dinner?"

There was a pause on the other end. "Both of us?"

"Yes—of course." He didn't want to talk to Valerie about their issues over the phone, so he kept it short. "Does five thirty work?"

"Yes. We can be there at five thirty. Can I bring something?"

"I have everything covered. You don't need to worry about bringing anything."

"Okay. We'll see you then."

"Bye."

Wade hit the red icon on his phone and put it back on the charging station. His hands were shaking, and he felt like he had just been through a boxing match. But as hard as that phone call had been, it wouldn't be nearly as hard as the conversation he needed to have with Valerie when she and Hailey came over.

"Is she coming?" Issy asked.

"Yes. They'll be here at five thirty."

"Yay!" Issy began to do a silly dance as she ran down the hall toward her room. "I need to get busy preparing for my guest!"

Despite the pain and uncertainty, Wade smiled.

He, too, needed to get ready for his guest. But it was his heart and mind he needed to prepare. He just prayed he hadn't ruined everything.

Chapter Fifteen

Snow began to fall as Valerie drove the car toward Wade's house. She and Hailey had left her mom at home for the evening, but she said she was happy to stay behind with a good book and some tea. She had encouraged Valerie to take Hailey to the Griffins', because she could see how miserable both of them were.

The days since her mom's arrival and Wade's reaction to the news had felt endless. The Christmas break that Valerie had been anticipating for weeks now felt hollow. She had enjoyed her time with her mom and daughter, but she had missed

Wade more than she expected. Every time she thought of him—and it was often—she ached with longing.

But his phone call hadn't been promising. He'd said that Issy wanted Hailey to come over. He hadn't said that he wanted her to come over. He'd invited her to join her daughter, but had it been out of obligation? Part of her tried to rationalize and admit that he hadn't needed to call at all. But the other part felt completely irrational.

Hailey was grinning in the back seat. She'd been so excited all afternoon, counting down the hours until they could leave for Issy's house.

Valerie had almost dreaded it. Not because she didn't want to see Wade, but because she was afraid it would be awkward when she did. How long could she bear awkward silence before it was appropriate to leave?

They pulled into his driveway, admiring the red-and-white Christmas lights he had used to line the eaves of his house. A bright green wreath hung on the side with a red bow.

Darkness had fallen almost an hour ago, but the glow of the lights brightened the snow around his house.

Valerie took a deep breath, second-guessing this plan. She had so much to say, but would Wade be willing to listen?

Hailey didn't hesitate. She jumped out of the car and ran to the front door where she pressed the doorbell before Valerie was even out of her vehicle. She had brought Annabelle—even though the dog hadn't been invited—and she had to take her out of the back seat.

Issy answered the door in seconds, apparently just as excited to see Hailey. The two embraced, as if they'd been separated for years instead of days.

Valerie approached the house carrying Annabelle as Wade appeared in the foyer. The girls ran off and Brayden rounded the corner. Wade had to lift an arm out of his son's way.

"You brought Annabelle!" Brayden said.

The little dog wiggled and squirmed to be let down, so Valerie obliged. She ran up to Brayden, barking with excitement.

Apparently, she had missed Brayden as much as Hailey had missed Issy and Valerie had missed Wade.

"Annabelle!" Brayden said as he giggled. "You came!" He took the dog and went into the house without another word, leaving Wade standing at the door and Valerie standing in the snow.

They studied each other and Valerie held her breath. Whatever was said in the next couple of minutes could determine the course of the rest of her life—for good or bad.

"I'm sorry," Valerie said, her breath puffing out from her mouth. She tried not to cry as she said, "I didn't intend to hurt you or anyone else. I wanted you to know— every day I wanted to tell you. But I had to honor Hailey's wishes, too. She had just told me the night before the pageant that I could finally tell you—but things happened beyond my control. I didn't want you to find out the way you did." She wiped at the traitorous tear that had escaped and trailed down her cheek.

Wade slowly stepped outside and closed the door behind him. He was wearing shoes, but not a coat or hat. He looked dear—so very dear—as he walked down the steps and met her in the driveway.

The lights from the house illuminated behind him, but she could still see his handsome face. His blue eyes were so intent as he stopped in front of her.

"I'm sorry, too, Valerie," he said. "I handled the situation poorly and brought past pains to the current situation. That wasn't fair to you."

More tears fell, and this time, she didn't bother to wipe them away. She wanted him to know everything. "I'm not proud of the past mistakes I've made. I got pregnant with Hailey while I was a senior in high school, and I thought it would be easiest to have my mom raise her as her daughter. At the time, it was—but over the years, the pain grew so intense, I worked harder and harder to try and push it away. I felt guilt and shame and I longed to know my daughter. I had no idea my mom was going to drop her off at my house out of the blue. Looking back, I wish I could have changed how it happened—but I'm not sorry it did happen. I love having Hailey in my life and I will never turn my back on her again."

He lifted his hand and paused before he gently wiped away her tears. His thumb was warm and soft as it caressed her skin.

She placed her hand over his, never wanting to let him go again. "Will you forgive me, Wade?"

"Of course, Valerie. But I'm asking you to forgive me, too."

"You didn't even have to ask." She knew she was risking everything by whispering the next words, but she'd already laid bare her soul. "I love you."

He caught his breath as he gazed deeply into her eyes. "You love me?"

She nodded, swallowing the emotions racing up her throat. "With all my heart."

He stepped closer to her and put his free hand at the small of her back, drawing her near to him. "I love you, too, Valerie."

His words felt like a sweet balm to her broken heart, soothing and healing. She was overcome with a sense of awe that this man, this good, kind and thoughtful man would love her.

"I've wanted to kiss you for weeks," he whispered as he drew her closer still.

"I've wanted to be kissed," she said, smiling as she lifted her face to his.

He lowered his lips to hers, enveloping them in a sweet, passionate kiss. She wrapped her arms around him, savoring every moment, in wonder that this was the first of countless kisses to come. She loved Wade Griffin and didn't want to be parted again.

He deepened the kiss, sending shivers up her spine, and she responded, so hungry for his love and affection that she didn't notice the cold or the snow. She was warmed by his touch, by the gentleness in his kiss and by the passion that reverberated between them.

When he finally pulled back, he offered her the most beautiful smile she'd ever seen. "I made two big mistakes the other night. One was walking away from you and the other was resigning my position as the music teacher. Is it too late?"

She shook her head, returning his smile. "Consider the resignation rescinded. I want you to teach at the school for as long as you want to be there. It might not always be easy to work together, but there are other couples who do."

Wade leaned his forehead against hers. "Does this mean we're a couple?"

"Do you want to be a couple?" she asked.

He kissed her again, this time with more passion and depth, and she was breathless when he was done.

"Is that a yes?" she asked with a laugh.

He drew her into his embrace and held her tight. "It's a yes." Then he took her hand and led her into the house. "I wish it wasn't so cold. I'd stay outside all night with you and keep you all to myself. I'm not sure how the kids will feel if they see me kissing you—which I intend to do several more times before you leave tonight."

Her cheeks felt warm as she grinned. "They're going to have to get used to it."

He closed the door behind her, and they stood in the dark foyer for a moment. "They might think it's strange that their dad is kissing their principal."

She stood on tiptoe and kissed him this time. "Not as strange as their principal kissing their dad."

He laughed as he hugged her close.

The air smelled like garlic and basil and when they finally entered the kitchen, all three kids were busy getting the supper dishes out of the cupboard to set the table.

"We saw you kissing in the snow," Issy said with a giggle.

"You saw?" Wade asked as he took Valerie's hand in his. "And what do you think? Are you guys okay if Valerie is my girlfriend?"

"Girlfriend?" Issy asked. "I want her to be your wife!"

Brayden and Hailey cheered at that idea and Valerie stepped close to Wade, wrapping her free hand around his arm.

"I think that means they're okay with their dad kissing their principal."

"Good," he said and he kissed her again. "Because I'm going to be doing it all the time."

The kids laughed and Brayden made a face—but Valerie knew that they were happy to see their dad and Hailey's mom together.

"Let's eat," Wade said. "I'm starving."

He let go of Valerie's hand to help the

kids. She placed her hand over her heart, knowing that she would never be the same again. And she was overjoyed.

The week slipped by with incredible speed. Wade woke up each morning with a grin on his face and he didn't stop smiling until he closed his eyes to sleep at night. Christmas morning, he and the children had gone to Valerie's to eat brunch and he had spent time getting to know her mom, Pam. When it was time for Pam to return to the Twin Cities to catch her flight, so she could be back in Arizona before night's end to spend part of Christmas Day with her husband, Wade invited Valerie and Hailey to have Christmas dinner with his parents and sister.

The evening had been full of laughter, food and games. And when it was time to leave, he didn't want it to end. He and Valerie made plans to take the kids sledding the next day, and the day after that, they went ice-skating. Each day that week, between Christmas and New Year's, they spent together. And with every passing day, he was more and more certain that he'd found the woman he wanted to spend the rest of his life with.

As he drove up to her house on New Year's Eve with the kids in the car, his heart was beating hard with excitement.

"Did you bring the ring, Daddy?" Issy asked from the backseat.

"It's in my pocket, Bug," he reassured her for the third time since leaving the house. "But don't say a word. Promise?"

"We promise," both kids chimed in.

Wade knew telling his children his plans to propose to Valerie was a risk—but he had wanted them to feel like they were part of the decision. He had taken them to the jeweler, and they had helped him pick out the ring that very afternoon. He knew it was fast—and that he and Valerie had only really known each other for a couple of months, but he knew everything he needed. He loved her more than life itself, and they had spent hours talking about their pasts—and discussing their hopes and dreams for the future. She had been open and honest about everything, no matter how painful, and he had done the same. He knew, deep within, that he wanted to spend the rest of his life with Valerie Wilmington, and he couldn't wait for the rest of his life to begin.

They pulled up to Valerie's house as the sun was just setting on the horizon, causing the entire sky to turn a soft shade of pink. The snow was piled high on the edges of the sidewalk, and more was forecasted for overnight.

Wade's pulse was beating hard as he stepped out of his truck.

Issy's eyes were wide with excitement, and she kept giggling.

"Not a word, Isabel," he warned.

She sobered and nodded. He rarely used her full name.

They walked up the sidewalk and Valerie was at the door to open it for them.

"Happy New Year's Eve," she said with a smile.

He kissed her, the weight of the ring in his pocket ever present. "Happy New Year's Eve," he whispered.

The kids ran into the house and Hailey was there to greet them. She said they were baking cookies and Issy joined her while Brayden started to play with Annabelle.

Wade hadn't considered how he'd propose to Valerie—if he'd make it a big gesture or do something casual. He trusted that the moment would come when it was supposed to—as long as Issy didn't spill the beans.

"Are you hungry?" Valerie asked as they stepped into the living room, and she closed the door behind him.

"Starving."

"Good. I made some beef stew and fresh bread. Hailey wants to make popcorn later. She is begging to stay up for midnight, but I don't think she'll make it."

"My kids, either. I had them bring their pajamas."

Valerie had already invited the kids to spend the night, since they would be staying so late. Wade would go home alone after midnight, but he didn't mind. He would come back early tomorrow for breakfast.

He hung up his jacket, conscious of the ring inside the box.

They spent the evening laughing around the supper table and then they played games with the kids. Hailey and Issy were determined to stay up until midnight, but Brayden made no such claims. He asked if he could sleep with Annabelle and was happy to go to sleep in the guest bedroom at the top of the stairs. Wade and Valerie tucked him into bed and Wade prayed for him as Valerie plugged in a night-light.

Brayden snuggled into bed with Annabelle happily under his arm.

"I could get used to this," Wade said to

Valerie as they closed the door and stood in the dark hallway.

"I could, too," she whispered as she kissed him.

The girls managed to stay up until just after eleven, but when both of them began to fall asleep on the couch as they watched *How the Grinch Stole Christmas!*, Wade sent Valerie a knowing glance.

"Come on," Valerie said to Hailey as she lifted her daughter off the couch. "It's time for bed."

"No," Hailey protested as she wrapped her arms around Valerie's neck. "I want to stay..." Her words faded as she fell asleep in Valerie's arms.

Wade scooped up Issy and followed Valerie up the stairs to Hailey's bedroom. They tucked the girls into Hailey's full-size bed and prayed for them before they left them to go back downstairs.

Valerie turned off the television and grabbed a blanket from a wicker basket in the corner while Wade went to his coat and slipped the ring into his hands.

His pulse had escalated again, but he knew that this was the moment he'd been waiting for. Their children were an important part of their life, but their marriage, if she was willing, would outlast their parenting. Once the children were grown, it would just be the two of them, and he wanted his proposal to be between them—and them alone.

She went to the couch, and he joined her, wrapping his arm around her as she pulled a blanket onto their laps. She laid her head on his shoulder.

The Christmas tree glowed as they sat next to each other. Wade kissed the top of Valerie's head, savoring this beautiful moment. He'd never felt more secure in a decision he'd made, and he was eager to see if she felt the same way.

"I don't want to leave," he said.

"It's not midnight. You don't need to leave yet."

"I mean, I don't want to leave at midnight or any time after that."

She looked up at him, studying him in the dim light. "I don't want you to leave, either. I love how it feels to have you and the kids all under one roof."

He kissed her and said, "It feels right—complete."

Wade slipped his hand into his pocket and gently pulled out the ring. He held it in front of her and she slowly sat up.

He took her hand and met her gaze. "I'm in love with you, Valerie Wilmington, and I know I will be until the day I die. We've only known each other a short time, but in that time, I've found you to be the most amazing woman I've ever known. I want to spend the rest of my life getting to know you. I want to grow with you and explore this wonderful life God has given us. Will you become my wife?"

She stared at him, tears gathering in her eyes. "Yes," she simply said, smiling with all the assurance he'd ever need.

He slipped the ring onto her left ring finger, and it fit perfectly.

"Wade, it's gorgeous."

"Issy insisted it's the one you'd love."

"She was right." She leaned forward and kissed him. When she pulled back, she said, "I'm so thankful for you and the kids. I didn't know what my life was missing until I met you—and now I can't imagine it any other way. I love you, too, with all my heart, and I can't wait to become your wife."

She snuggled back into his side, laying her head on his shoulder as she lifted her hand and looked at the ring. It sparkled in the glow of the Christmas lights.

Wade admired it with her, loving how it looked on her finger—and loving, even more, what it meant.

He had found his happily-ever-after and he had realized it began the moment he met Valerie.

Chapter Sixteen

Sunshine broke through the clouds as Valerie, Hailey and Issy entered Timber Falls Community Church from the back entrance that cold January day. Valerie was wearing a simple white gown, long and sleek with tight sleeves and a scooped neckline. Hailey and Issy were wearing soft pink dresses with sparkling skirts. They had chosen them together, and their decision had been unanimous.

"We're going to be sisters today," Issy said to Hailey with a squeal of delight.

Liv Harris was there. As their wedding planner and Valerie's friend. She was waiting at the door for Valerie and the girls.

"We're ready to get started!" Liv said with an excited smile. "Wade and Brayden are in the sanctuary and all your guests have arrived."

Valerie's nerves were overshadowed by her happiness. She'd never known such joy as this day brought—and she hadn't even seen Wade yet.

Issy had stayed the night at Valerie's after the rehearsal and groom's dinner, and they had spent the morning getting ready together. Valerie's house was stacked with boxes that would be brought to Wade's as soon as their honeymoon ended. They had decided to live in Wade's house, since it was twice as big as Valerie's. She would miss her home, but she was excited to begin a new life with Wade and the children in his house. The backyard and the Mississippi River were hard to resist, and the neighborhood was tucked away, near the golf course, which also made it more appealing to raise the children.

But those things were in the back of Valerie's mind as she stood in the hallway and took a deep breath. The pictures of all the other couples that had been married at Timber Falls Community Church, or by Pastor Jake, hung on the wall. Valerie knew many of the recent couples. Chase and Joy Asher, Jake and Kate Dawson, Max and Piper Evans, Zane and Liv Harris, Knox and Merritt Taylor, Nate and Adley Marshall, Drew and Whitney Keelan, Clay and Emma Foster, and Will and Jessa Madden. She'd heard some of their stories and looked forward to hearing others. But it felt good to be among so many people who had such happy marriages— she hoped and prayed that it would be an indicator of her own happiness, though she knew that her marriage was up to her and Wade alone.

"Ready?" Liv asked.

"Almost." Valerie turned when the door opened, and her mom entered. She was wearing a navy blue mother-of-the-bride gown, and she looked a little breathless as she handed Valerie her bouquet.

"Sorry," Valerie said as she accepted the bouquet and turned back to Liv. "I forgot it in the car and my mom ran back for it." She took a deep breath and grinned. "I'm ready now."

She was more than ready to become Mrs. Griffin. She and Wade had planned a quick weekend getaway to Stillwater, Minnesota, a charming town near the Twin Cities, and would take the kids on an extended vacation that summer when they were off school. Wade's parents had agreed to stay at Wade's house for the weekend to keep an eye on them and Valerie's mom and Lyle would stay at her house.

"Let's go," Liv said as she led them toward the sanctuary doors, which were closed.

Hailey and Issy stood in front of Valerie, while her mom stood at her side. She would give Valerie away.

Liv nodded at the two ushers who were

standing at the ready, and when the doors opened, the music inside the sanctuary shifted to "Canon in D."

The congregation, consisting mostly of friends and neighbors, stood to their feet. Valerie saw several of her students and their parents, as well as all the couples she'd noted in the hallway. Wade's extended family had come and a few of Valerie's friends from college and her other jobs.

But, most important, was Wade.

He stood at the front of the church and turned as the others rose to their feet.

Their gazes met as Valerie began to walk down the aisle with her mother at her side.

Tears gathered in her eyes as she smiled at her groom. Warmth and affection filled her as they watched one another.

Not for the first time, she marveled at God's gift. She didn't deserve Wade's love, yet he had offered it to her. Just like Hailey's love, Valerie would never take Wade's love for granted. It was a gift, something to be treasured and cared for. She would nourish it and watch it grow, praying that it would be a blessing to them, to their children and to all their friends and family.

When she arrived at the front, Pastor Jake was there with Wade and Brayden.

Hailey and Issy stepped to the side and Pastor Jake said, "Who gives this woman to be married to this man?"

At the same moment, Hailey, Issy, Brayden and Valerie's mom said, "We do."

The congregation chuckled, but several people became teary-eyed as her mom gave Valerie a hug and then stepped back to join Lyle in the front pew.

Valerie smiled at Wade as he took her hand and drew her to his side.

They faced Pastor Jake as he addressed the congregation, but all Valerie was aware of was Wade. His smell, the strength of his hand, holding hers, and the feel of his body as he pressed against her—as if he'd never let her go.

The kids stood close, their little family

uniting as one for the rest of their lives. To have and to hold from this day forward, for better, for worse, for richer, for poorer, in sickness and in health, to love and to cherish, they would be a family. Sisters and brother, mother and father, son and daughters. Their roles and titles were changing, but in the most wonderful way possible. Valerie marveled at it all, holding it in her heart, pondering the meaning and beauty of it all.

And when the vows were spoken, the rings exchanged and the promises made, Pastor Jake said, "I now pronounce you husband and wife. What God has brought together, let no man put asunder. You may kiss your bride, Wade."

Valerie turned to her husband, the weight of her new wedding band hugging her finger like a gentle embrace. She lifted her face to him, all the love and joy she felt reflected in his eyes.

He kissed her—and the audience cheered.

Hailey and Issy giggled, and Brayden rolled his eyes—but he smiled, too.

"You're my wife," Wade said to Valerie, for her ears alone.

"Forever and always," she said.

"Promise?" he asked.

"With all my heart."

Wade smiled at her and kissed her again. Then they faced their friends and family and they cheered.

Valerie didn't know that such happiness existed—not until today.

* * * * *

If you liked this story from Gabrielle Meyer, check out her previous Love Inspired books:

Available now from Love Inspired!

Find more great reads at www.LoveInspired.com.

Dear Reader,

I have loved creating the fictional town of Timber Falls, modeled closely after my own hometown of Little Falls. Many of the businesses, homes and landscape are very real. The downtown, the parks and the Mississippi River are all part of the beauty of where I live. It's so much fun to see some of the couples from previous stories make cameo appearances, while introducing new characters to the community. It's easy for me to imagine all of them and their lives as they revolve around Timber Falls Community Church and the adjoining school. Thank you for coming along on the journey. I hope you've enjoyed this latest installment in the Timber Falls series.

Blessings,
Gabrielle Meyer